BLOOD RED BLUES

BLOOD RED BLUES

A HARLEM NOIR
INTRODUCING DEVIL BARNETT

TEDDY HAYES

KATE'S MYSTERY BOOKS
JUSTIN, CHARLES & CO., PUBLISHERS
BOSTON

FIRST U.S. EDITION 2004

Originally published in 1998 by The X Press, London

This is a work of fiction. All characters and events portrayed
in this work are either fictitious or are used fictitiously.

ISBN: 1-932112-21-9

Library of Congress Cataloging-in-Publication Data is available.

Published in the United States by Kate's Mystery Books,
an imprint of Justin, Charles & Co., Publishers,
20 Park Plaza, Boston, Massachusetts 02116
www.justincharlesbooks.com

Distributed by National Book Network
Lanham, Maryland
www.nbnbooks.com

1 2 3 4 5 6 7 8 9 10

Printed in the United States of America

To
Jennie Rosenthal

BLOOD RED BLUES

*C*hina Blue was almost six feet tall. Long straight hair flowed across her slim, pale shoulders, cascading into a silky jet-black mane. The thick layer of green mascara outlining a pair of hazel-brown eyes gave her the look of a glazed oriental ceramic cat poised in the window of a Chinese curio shop. The vice squad had China Blue listed as Setsuko Nakamora — prostitute and shoplifter.

Marijuana smoke floated through the air as China Blue fucked with a fat Colombian named Jesus on the couch. A prostitute named Esther lay naked against the several soft, furry pillows on the floor. Mr. Yamaguchi, a bespectacled Japanese businessman in his early forties, sat watching them from a nearby over-stuffed chair. He blinked his popped eyes steadily and smiled mechanically as if someone had dropped a coin into a slot on the top of his head. Esther moaned louder and louder each time the man thrust himself inside her. Mr. Yamaguchi toyed with the waistband of his baggy boxer shorts and waited for Peter Pan to re-enter the room. Peter Pan was his date, and in the deep recesses of his mind he had decided to make her moan like Esther. The thought of it extended his erection. Mr. Yamaguchi usually didn't even like black girls; he generally preferred blondes. But this one was so cute he just couldn't resist. Besides, he had business in Harlem, so he figured that he might as well sample the neighborhood's merchandise while he was on the job.

The man pumped faster and faster until Esther let out an ear-piercing scream of ecstasy. She slid her thick juicy lips along the man's ear and bit him lightly at the base of his neck.

"Oh, Paaaaapy!" she wailed. She shuddered, then went limp like a rag doll in the arms of the man whose eyes seemed dead inside of his face.

On the other side of the room, Jesus was fondling China Blue. Esther's noisy orgasm had broken his concentration. Jesus was rich. He sold cocaine for a living. He grinned over at Esther, rubbing the folds of his huge belly in anticipation.

"We can switch now, okay?" the Colombian suggested to the man with the expressionless eyes as he greedily licked his chops and eyed Esther's big, round, creamy buttocks.

Peter Pan sauntered into the room wearing a black negligee and smoking a joint. She didn't look a day over seventeen. She passed the reefer around and lit a new one for herself. The man with the dead eyes took a hit from the joint. He inhaled deeply, then blew the smoke directly into Esther's mouth. Jesus left the room and returned with a large, square mirror sprinkled with twelve lines of cocaine.

"A little something for my special friends." He said as he passed the cocaine around.

China Blue fished a rolled-up twenty-dollar bill from her purse on the table and took the first hit. Mr. Yamaguchi made little grunting noises when he snorted, which made everyone laugh. One line was all Yamaguchi needed to pull out his penis and start screwing Peter Pan in the middle of the floor.

After the second line of coke the man with the dead eyes pulled China Blue from the sofa onto the floor and started doing the 69. He had barely gotten into his rhythm when an almighty crash splintered the front door into a thousand pieces.

A big, barrel-chested Asian man wielding a sledgehammer pushed his way through the splinters like a Sherman tank. A smaller version of the first wearing a black eye-patch and holding a 9mm automatic in his hand followed. Naked and confused, Mr. Yamaguchi raised his hands in surrender. Effortlessly, the bigger of the two Asian men hoisted the man with the dead eyes up from between China Blue's legs and flung him across the room like a sack of potatoes. Then he turned his attention to China Blue.

The crowd gathered in front of the Tease Me Club on 125th Street and Lenox were watching the last of the ambulances drive away when I pulled up. I parked at 123rd and walked back. As I approached, uniformed policemen were breaking up the crowd.

"Okay. It's all over," one tall black cop was yelling to the bystanders in an agitated voice, "you all can go home now, the fun's over."

I headed for the entrance of the club along with a group of others.

"What's up?" I asked a guy in front.

"Bodies, about five of 'em," a face from under a greasy Giants baseball cap informed me.

"More like six or seven," someone else chimed in.

Nobody seemed to have any real details. Just that there had been gunshots.

"Lord, I need me a drink, this killing messin' with my nerves," an aging hooker declared, heading for the bar.

"Hey, yo, I seen it all," a crack-head shouted to a young white man with a Channel 5 news camera on his shoulder.

"You were up there?" the newsman asked and swung the camera in the direction of the crack-head.

"Yeah. Give me fifty dollars, I'll give you the real story chief, make you famous," the crack-head answered.

"Get the hell outta here," the policeman yelled at the crack-head, pointing his Billy club in the drug addict's direction.

The crack-head backed away.

"Damn, man, why you wanna go and hurt a brotha?" he complained.

"Come on, come on," shouted the black cop, now joined by two nervous-looking white colleagues.

I had come to "The Tease" on business, so amid all the activity I quietly slipped through the crowd and made my way inside the club.

The Tease Me Club was a like a hundred other bars in Harlem. Then again, it wasn't like any other bar in Harlem. The Tease, as it was more commonly known, was a go-go club with nude exotic dancing, designed like a cave and decorated in earth colors, with the kind of lighting that made almost anyone with any shade of brown skin look desirable. Its jukebox was strictly funky. A long narrow bar ran half the length of the room. Further towards the back was a main stage, which rose about four feet off the floor with tables on three sides. Booney, the bouncer, stood six feet nine, weighed three hundred and twenty pounds, and looked like a mean giant Buddha. He sat over in the corner near the door picking his teeth and watching a thin, tan girl, naked except for a G-string and a garter, twisting on the stage. The regulars were a mix of local politicians, middle-aged businessmen, and old-time hustlers, most of whom had returned to their favorite haunt from which they had departed hastily the previous night when the police had descended. The dancers ranged in age from their mid-twenties to their early thirties. About half were black and the others were white, East Asian, and Hispanic. The locals called it The Poor Man's International Club. It was no secret, everybody who was anybody knew about the private apartments on the third floor where well-heeled sugardaddies and cops could rendezvous with the dancers and/or hookers of their choice. As I made my way to the bar, I inhaled a mix of cigarette smoke, alcohol, and cheap perfume.

"Devil Barnett, my man. How you be baby?"

I looked up. The voice belonged to my old friend Raymond Williams, one of the bartenders, a thin, light skinned man in his early thirties with a thick mustache. He was smiling widely.

"How you been keeping, dog? Ain't seen you since the funeral, you all right?"

"Yep, okay, mostly working, not much else," I answered.

"Good to keep busy, good," he said giving me a look of under-standing that conveyed his sharing of my recent grief. "What'll it be?"

"Scotch and water."

He nodded, turned, and grabbed a bottle of Dewars from the counter behind him. I eased myself onto a barstool.

"Listen, if you ever need any extra help, just call, I'll make the time," he offered.

"Thanks."

He finished pouring my drink and went to serve some cus-tomers at the other end of the bar.

I had come back home to Harlem a few months before, soon after my father had been murdered in a holdup at the Be-Bop Tavern, the bar he owned and managed for many years. Two teenage kids high on crack had come in to rob the place one night when my father was closing up. They had taken the money and were on their way out of the door when one of them got the bright idea that it would be better not to leave any witnesses be-hind, then blasted my father in the chest at point blank range with a sawed-off shotgun. When they caught the kid, he told the police he'd gotten the idea from a movie he had seen.

The long and short of it was that a man who had served his country and won a purple heart risking his life in the Korean War, a man who had helped to register black people in Harlem to vote each year for over twenty-five years, a man who had marched with Congressman Adam Clayton Powell down 125th street so that black people could work where they shopped, had gotten murdered at sixty-three years old for a five dollar bag of crack co-caine.

Rather than sell the bar, I quit my job at the Agency and re-turned home to run it. The bar trade wasn't anything new. I had worked at the Be-Bop through high school and college.

My business at The Tease was at the invitation of its manager, Honey Lavelle. I was to be inducted as a member of a select buy-ers' association for booze that happened to fall off the back of trucks with some regularity each month. Cases and cases of top shelf liquor. With business being as volatile as it often was in Harlem, sometimes the only way to make a decent profit was to cut corners here and there. More importantly, to be invited into this buyers' group was a sign of being trusted and accepted into the Harlem business and political network, a network moreover where one could gain access to the kind of information that could be useful to one's business, even strategic to one's survival. My father had been a member of the group. Now the torch was being passed along. Even though I had received the call from Honey Lavelle, the invitation had come from Honey's boss. Honey Lavelle didn't do anything unless it was okayed first by the Sultan, her boss, who was also my uncle.

I sipped my drink and watched two plain clothes cops come in. One was in his fifties, the other much younger. They entered, looked around, and sat at the bar. They were about as subtle as two turds in a punchbowl. In general, Harlemites were of the opinion that New York's Finest never did much to the benefit of anybody other than themselves. Black or white it didn't matter, a cop was a cop was a cop. And shit stank no matter where it came from. There was too much graft being paid and too many drug dealers operating in Harlem for anyone with a functioning brain to think otherwise.

The older cop asked Melvin, the head bartender, to take him into the back to see the manager, while the other, a clean-shaven babyfaced black guy in his late twenties wearing jeans, a sweat-shirt, and a leather jacket, sat at the bar and attempted to blend in with the crowd.

On stage, a few young women clad in revealing mini skirts were warming the place up with a little bump and grind.

"I know she in here. I know it." A booming voice cut through from the back room, as loud as a bullhorn.

"I need to talk to Seven Up," blurted a small, scrawny black man in his late forties, with a three-day-old gray flecked beard, as he staggered up to the bar.

"She ain't here. She'll be back later," Raymond said, trying to placate him and hoping the drunk didn't find the person he was looking for.

"I need to talk to her now, goddammit," the man repeated, slamming his fist down hard on the bar.

Booney, the giant black Buddha, moved slowly from his perch with the smoothness and stealth of a Bengal tiger and eased up next to the irate customer. He whispered something into the little man's ear that seemed to calm him down. He gave the man a friendly pat on his shoulder then returned to his post at the end of the bar.

"Gimme a double, naw, make that a triple gin," the scrawny man demanded.

He wore a wrinkled green suit with a yellow and green polka dot tie. The collar of the soiled yellowish shirt was badly frayed, and his scuffed brown and yellow oxfords looked as if they'd never seen a shoe shine. But at least he was color-coordinated.

I sipped my drink and waited for Honey as another girl mounted the stage. She announced herself as Seven Up and started to move with about half as much energy as the previous girl but with more rhythm and more experience. Her long brown legs rocked steadily to the drumbeat. She gyrated up close to one of the tables of men seated nearby on the floor below, and pulled her G String down so they could focus on the goodies contained inside. In appreciation of the view, the men stuffed paper currency into the red garter on her right thigh.

I watched two more dancers come and go and drank as many drinks, occasionally checking out the undercover cop drinking ginger ale and trying to act normal. Then out of the blue the little scrawny drunk guy in the green suit jumped up on the bar and began to shout.

"Bitch!" he screamed in a grating voice, almost drowning out the music.

Blam!

The unmistakable sound of a gunshot made everyone dive for

cover. The little man with the gray flecked whiskers was waving a .44 magnum, with tears streaming down his ebony-hued face.

"If I can't have you then can't nobody else either," he yelled.

Booney stood silent and motionless, poised and ready to strike.

"I mean what I say," the man cried, his chest heaving.

The commotion brought Honey Lavelle out of her back office. Seven Up stood trembling.

"Herman," Honey's voice was cool and controlled as she called across the room in the man's direction. "Put that damn gun away and come down from there, you're drunk."

"I may be drunk, goddammit, but I know one goddamn thing, I'm gonna blow me and her both to kingdom come, right here tonight, if she don't say she love me like I love her."

Herman pointed the gun at Seven Up. He aimed high, then cocked the hammer and fired twice. He missed twice. Most of the patrons were still under the tables, not counting those who had made it to the door. The jukebox was playing Marvin Gaye's "Give It Up."

"See, I'll do it, I mean it," he said and shot into the ceiling once more for effect. "I got two shots left, one for me and one for her. Either she take my wedding ring right now or, I swear to God, I'll do it."

Seven Up, who looked young naturally, appeared even younger with terror in her eyes.

Honey looked at the pathetic little man and sighed. "Okay Herman, come down from there and give me the goddamn ring, and let's have your wedding right here and now."

"Right here, now?" repeated Herman swaying in place under the influence of the liquor.

"Right here, now I said," Honey echoed.

"But don't we need a preacher?"

"We got our own preacher, Booney," she said and pointed to the giant black bouncer.

"Booney is a preacher? I didn't know that. Well I'll be durn." Herman was astounded.

From the look of confusion that registered on Booney's face, he hadn't known it either.

"Come on Seven Up and marry your new husband," Honey insisted.

"This ain't no trick is it?" asked Herman showing doubt for the first time. "Cause if it is, I'll kill you too."

"Do you wanna marry this girl or not?" asked Honey.

"Sho I do, I love her."

"Well let's go then."

Herman climbed carefully down off the bar and moved next to his seat. He still held the gun trained on Seven Up though.

As the undercover cop reached for the pistol in the small of his back, I eased up next to him and whispered in his ear. "It's okay officer, Honey's got it under control. I know her and him. Just be cool."

He glared at me.

"I'm a law enforcement officer, it's okay," I assured.

I had learned during my years as a CIA operative that a cop will listen to another cop more readily than he would Jesus himself. There were also a lot of other things I had learned as an agent. Most of which I hoped to forget by leaving the Agency and coming back to Harlem and trying to live a normal life.

The cop relaxed a bit, but still kept his hand on his holstered gun.

Booney followed Honey who led Seven Up by the hand into the middle of the room, like a lamb to the slaughter. While his bride-to-be bawled her eyes out, Herman was smiling like a fool. With his gun still pointed at Seven Up, Herman affected a snaggle-toothed grin and gently kissed his bride-to-be. He was attempting to clear his head and bring some dignity to the occasion when Honey winked a signal to Booney. Herman never saw it coming.

Booney's big meaty fist cracked into the side of Herman's jaw with the force of a jackhammer, causing him to bite off the tip of his tongue. Somewhere in his mind, Herman may have thought he heard angels singing, because for him everything went black. With Herman lying knocked out on the floor, the world had become a safer place.

"Sorry about the disturbance, people," Honey announced to the room. "Everyone gets a free round on the house."

The various patrons spoke their approval and resumed their places at the tables and the bar. Almost simultaneously the jukebox blared out a new number. This time it was the Temptations' "Poppa Was A Rolling Stone." Across the room, Honey motioned me to follow her into the back. The young undercover cop followed Booney, who had thrown Herman across his huge shoulders and was carrying him out of The Tease.

"You sure everything is okay, Miss?" the undercover cop asked Honey as he departed.

"I'm fine," Honey said identifying him immediately as a cop. "It ain't no big thing, he pulls that act on some poor girl about once every six months. Just part of the entertainment. I'm used to it."

"If he's done that before, why don't you file charges or better still, why don't you just bar him from the place?" the cop suggested.

"Ain't that easy," she told him. "He's one of our best customers. Besides, my mother wouldn't like it. He's my uncle."

Honey Lavelle's office was decorated in brown and black. It had a tan rug that matched the curtains, two rust colored cushioned chairs, a black bookcase, and a black desk. The walls were covered with framed civic awards handed out by different neighborhood organizations like the NAACP, The Urban League, and The Mayor's Minority Business Council. Two large framed prints of autumn country scenes, showing a pretty lake with ducks flying off into the sunset, adorned the same wall. On the other side of the room there were two large black filing cabinets and a mahogany cart with wheels that held a serving tray filled with a variety of liquors, an ice bucket, and six glasses.

"Crazy people don't know how to act decent," Honey frowned and sat down in her high-backed black chair facing me. "Sorry you had to come at such a bad time," she apologized.

"Don't worry about it. So what happened? When I came in, out front was crawling with cops."

"Not sure yet. Six bodies dusted with cocaine. May have been a drug hit. The Sultan just found out and he's ready to come down on somebody with both feet. Looks like it might be me."

A slight look of worry crept into her pretty features.

"By the way, lock that door for me, I was just in the middle of something before my old drunk ass uncle started acting a fool."

I got up and turned the bolt on one of two brass locks on the inside of the office door. As I turned back into the room, Honey was lifting one of the prints with the autumn scenes off the wall. Behind it was a one way mirror that looked into the office next to hers. Below the one way mirror was a small speaker with a red button for volume control. Looking into the next room we could see and hear the older plainclothes cop questioning Melvin, the bartender, about what had happened upstairs earlier.

Melvin Hodges was sixty years old, tall and lanky, with a full head of gray hair. He sat stooped over and wore thick-rimmed black glasses. He was sitting on a hardback chair looking dutifully attentive while the agitated undercover cop paced the floor smoking a cigarette with one hand and patting a black spiral notebook on the side of his leg with the other. His worried expression showed that he was under pressure to get some answers. The only problem was, murder or no murder, this was still Sultan's territory. And nobody would say anything unless he told them to. It was the same all over Harlem. Because Harlem was the kind of place where a man's foot could slip, and in doing so he might lose his soul. Melvin was being cool. Giving the cop all his attention but no real information.

"Did you know the person who rented the place?" the cop asked.

"Yes," Melvin answered slowly, exaggerating his southern drawl to appear harmless and not so smart. "It was a woman named China Blue, I believe."

"She a regular?"

"Regular, sir?"

"Does she come here regularly as a customer?" the cop repeated.

"She dances here sometimes."

"How long has she been a dancer here?"

"Off and on maybe two years, yeah, maybe two years, can't be sure though."

"Did you know her to be a drug dealer or to be involved with drugs?" The cop was desperately trying to establish some link that would help him build a case.

"No, sir."

Melvin was acting exactly as he had been trained to act, cautious and courteous at all times, and giving away only information that was already in the public domain. In the twenty years he had worked at The Tease, he had become an old hand at cooperating with the police. Tell 'em everything without telling them anything.

"Did you give her the key?" the cop wanted to know.

"Yes, sir."

"What time was that?"

"Around eight."

"Did she sign a receipt for it?"

"She did. Yes, sir."

As Melvin answered his questions, the cop jotted in the notebook.

"Anyone else with her when she picked up the key?"

"Not that I saw, sir."

"Did you know her to be a prostitute?"

"No, sir."

"Well didn't you ever talk to the woman, didn't you know anything about her?"

"No, sir."

"Mr. Hodges, you mean to sit here and tell me that this woman, who rented your upstairs room for a party and who was brutally murdered, worked here for two years and you didn't know anything about her?" the cop raised his voice in exasperation.

"Officer, I work here as a bartender. I am a professional. It is the policy of the management that male staff do not get personal with any of the womenfolk who work here. I needs my job and I likes my job, so I follow the rules," Melvin said exaggerating his best country boy act.

"Did you take any drinks up to the room?" the policeman grimaced.

"No, she ordered something and took it with her when she got the key."

"So after you heard shots, you went upstairs and discovered the dead bodies?"

Melvin paused. He considered his thoughts, then his words.

"I didn't find no dead bodies."

"I thought you told me before, you went up and found the dead bodies."

"No, sir," Melvin corrected. "I told you I heard shots and I went up to investigate. I then reported the problem to my manager, Miss

Lavelle, and she called the police. The police found the dead bodies. I was just with the police when they went into the room, sir."

The frustration was building up. The policeman let out a long and deep sigh.

"Did you see anyone else go up with her when she picked up the key from you, maybe Esther Fernandez?"

"No, sir, she was alone as far as I knew. I said that before."

"Well how did the other people get in?"

"Don't know. They could have come in through the rear entrance to the building and taken the back stairway, sir."

"Mr. Hodges, if I find out later that you've been lying to me it won't go down so easy with you, I'll see to that," the cop threatened.

"Mister, I can only tell you what I know, unless you want me to lie to you, which I wouldn't do anyway because I'm a Christian."

The undercover cop looked at Melvin, twisted his face, grunted, and put his notebook away.

"That's all Mr. Hodges, for now, thank you," the cop sneered. "By the way, would you call your boss and tell her we'd like to talk with her again."

Melvin picked up the phone that was sitting on the desk and dialed Honey's office. She answered on the second ring.

"Miss Lavelle, the officer questioning me said he would like to see you again," Melvin purposely stammered into the phone.

"Tell him, as soon as I get out of my meeting. Give him a drink while he's waiting," Honey replied.

Honey placed the print back on the wall and turned her attention back to me.

"Your choice," she offered, holding her hand out towards the bottles on the serving tray.

"Scotch."

"Ice?"

"Straight."

She poured one for me, and then poured a drink for herself from the same bottle and sat opposite me, looking into my face with eyes that had lost their businesslike edge. They were now the eyes of a woman looking at a man.

"So, Youngblood, how have you been keeping?" she opened the conversation as she folded her leg under her butt. She wore a green silk pantsuit that showed the curves of her figure. Though she was easily in her early forties, her body looked firm in all the right places. Her nails were done up tastefully in a soft pink tone that matched her lipstick. Honey was a pretty woman. The kind that was able to turn heads when she walked down the street. What's more, she was very aware of her sexual power and knew exactly how to use it.

"Tell me, how did you come by the name Devil?" she quipped in an offhanded way followed by a smile.

"It's a nickname that kinda stuck," I told her. "Long story, I'll tell you one day."

"Nickname, huh?" her voice trailed off as she let her gaze fall into her glass. She looked up again and spoke. "When you gonna let me get some of that," she asked straightforwardly and ran her eyes the length of my body. "You don't plan to run forever, do you?"

I didn't know what to say. She had caught me by surprise.

She threw her head back and laughed out loud. I could tell she liked getting a rise out of me. She took a swallow from her glass and I followed suit.

"Who says I've been running?"

"Actions speak louder than words, Youngblood. What's the matter, you don't go for older broads?"

She was still looking me square in the eyes and smiling.

"No, that's not it." I returned her look. "It's just that I haven't given much thought to my personal life since I've been back."

"I can imagine it's been rough huh?" The tone of her voice changed to reflect real concern.

"Yeah, but I've been making it okay."

"You know Mr. Ernest was my buddy. We used to talk sometimes when he came by. Your dad was a first-class guy. And he did me a solid or two over the years and I never got to pay him back fully. But the debt is still good, just want you to know."

"Thanks, it's good to know there's a place to come get a favor."

"And maybe a few other things too, if you decide to change your mind," she added, smiling again. "But you came here to talk about some other business if my memory serves me," she said, letting me off the hook.

"Yeah."

We talked about the cases of liquor that I could get at a forty percent discount off the regular price, about the cash payments, and about the dates and times of delivery. The whole conversation lasted less than ten minutes.

She walked back to the tray and freshened our drinks.

"Tell me, if it's not too personal, I know your father died, but you've been away all these years, so why did you decide to settle back in Harlem?"

I gave the only answer that had any ring of truth to it even though I didn't quite know if I understood it fully myself yet.

"Because this is home."

We looked straight at each other for what seemed like a long time in silence. She finished her drink then spoke in a calm, sincere voice.

"I like you, Youngblood. You've got a lot of Mr. Ernest in you."

"We're going to be friends," she said.

I walked to the corner of 123rd street where my car was parked and looked westward into the Harlem night. The full moon looked like a hundred-watt bulb burning in the purple sky. Even through the dusk I could still see the dirt and squalor that Harlem had become since my youth, and began to think about the question Honey had asked me. Why had I come back, here of all places? The more I looked around at the desolation, the more her words tugged at something inside of me. What Harlem had been when I was growing up and what Harlem had become seemed a world apart.

Yes, all the landmarks were still here. The Apollo Theatre, the home of all the famous black entertainers for over four decades, still stood supreme. The big beautiful churches were still here. So was the Harlem talk, and the Harlem walk, but that magic spirit in the hearts of the people that had made Harlem world famous had been somehow diminished. In its place was a kind of decay, eating the place alive from the inside out. Where was the spirit that had nurtured the genius of people like Duke Ellington, Malcolm X, Langston Hughes, James Baldwin, Chester Himes, Nipsy Russell, Hazel Scott, and Paul Robeson? Now, instead of the churches in Harlem being filled with men like Adam Clayton Powell, who preached political sermons from the pulpit, the black churches in Harlem were filled on Sunday mornings with busloads of European and Japanese tourists, who came to witness Harlem Negroes praising the Lord. One could almost hear the black preachers welcoming them in. "Let us play the music and pass the plate, chillun, 'cause everybody knows God needs more money for grass seed and water molecules, 'cause the price of everything is going up."

Yes, Harlem had changed. Where there had once been Charlie Parker and Dizzy Gillespie creating bebop jazz at Minton's Cafe, now there was gangsta rap music blaring from open jeeps. Rap music that offended womanhood, was being blasted in the ears of babies and grandmothers alike. Where there had once been small black businesses owned and run by Harlem residents, South East Asians from places like Vietnam and Korea had set up shops and sold cheap foreign-made goods to their black customers at a premium. The black-owned bank that had operated in Harlem since the 1920s had folded. The hope that had always been placed in the chance of a better job and higher education had been replaced by a despair associated with young drug dealers selling drugs to school children on the streets. There were more black politicians in Harlem now than there had ever been, yet black people here seemed worse off economically and politically than ever before.

I turned my car eastward and headed up the FDR Drive, still deep in thought. The fifteen years I had spent as a CIA operative hadn't meant much either. Like Harlem, at one point the job was shiny and new, and had sparked a spirit inside me, but over the years the magic and enthusiasm had become tarnished like exposed silverware in a damp basement.

I had been a field operative, a spy out in the cold. I guess I just got tired of the hypocrisy, the nigger jokes behind my back, having to listen to opinions from idiots with a tenth of my brain power telling me what to do. Maybe my homecoming had a lot to do with events that culminated all at once. What the Indians refer to as karma, or what Malcolm X called "the chickens coming home to roost." Maybe if I had stayed with the Agency for twenty more years, I would have crashed through the glass ceiling to become to the CIA what Colin Powell had become to the army during George Bush Senior's Administration. The first black man at the top of the heap. I knew how to play the game better than most but I guess I just got tired. Tired and lonely.

The loneliness of not having Amanda. Amanda. Sometimes just the thought of her would bring a dull pain up through my stomach to lodge in my chest. That's why I tried not to think about her. I promised myself I wouldn't ever again. But I still did. We had found something in each other that filled the emptiness we both knew. She had been my safe haven and I had been her healer.

Home is a four-story brownstone building near the corner of 155th, the same house I grew up in. When my grandmother was alive she lived on the main floor. We always rented out the basement floor to help with the mortgage. Our family, which consisted of just me and Dad after my mother died, lived on the top two floors. Now that my grandmother was dead, I rented out the main floor as well.

As I climbed the stairs to my second floor entrance I noticed how toasty it was in the hallway despite the October chill. The heat of the new boiler I had recently installed was apparently doing its job. Miss Mayberry, my tenant, was away in Georgia visiting her son. She was a senior citizen with arthritis. Maybe now her aging bones would have a chance of some relief at night. She would be away for the next month, so for now I had the whole place to myself.

My two floors had been newly redecorated. I had had the master bathroom remodeled and a Jacuzzi installed. There was new wallpaper and paint throughout. The color scheme was black and turquoise on the second floor and deep blue and magenta on the top floor. The second floor housed the living room, kitchen, and a spare bedroom. On the top floor were the master bedroom, bathroom, and a small room full of the latest computer equipment that I used as a home office.

I looked through the mail, separated the bills from the junk, turned on the stereo system, then went upstairs to check the answering machine. There were four calls. The first caller had hung up without leaving a message. The second was my head barmaid, Christine. The third call was from the service department at Appliance City saying that they needed the original receipt before they would honor the warranty to repair my refrigerator. The fourth caller had hung up without leaving a message.

Herbie Hancock's "Dis is Da Drum" oozed out of the stereo as I made my way into the kitchen for a tuna fish sandwich and a cup of herbal tea before kicking my feet up. I was starting to doze off when the doorbell rang. I reached for the nine millimeter from its resting place in the drawer of the china cabinet and slipped it into the waistband of my pants. Old habits are hard to break.

The peephole revealed two black men. Through the open-work brocaded lace pattern of the heavy curtains that covered the outer glass door I recognized the young plain clothes cop I had seen earlier that night at the Tease Me Club overdosing on ginger ale and trying to fit in to the ambiance. The other man I hadn't seen before. I relaxed.

"Mr. Barnett, Mr. Marcus Barnett?" the young cop asked as I opened the door. "I'm Officer Robert Evans of NYPD," he said holding out his badge. "I've been asked by my captain to stop by and see if you would accompany us to the precinct."

The other cop nodded his hello. I nodded back.

"Suppose I say no?"

"W-w-well," Evans stammered. "Sir it, would place me in an awkward position. This is strictly informal and strictly by request. I was told to mention the name Deke Robinson if you had any objections. My captain said that you were a friend of his. Mr. Robinson I mean, not the captain."

"Okay, give me a minute." I closed the door.

I returned the gun to the cabinet, pulled on a thick sweater, and put on a jacket. The night air had chilled and I thought that maybe it might rain. I considered putting on a heavier jacket because drastic changes in the weather can present serious health problems for me, as it does for every carrier of the sickle-cell anemia disease. For a long time now I had been able to have some control over the disease, partly because I took good care of myself and partly because I had trained myself to deal positively with stressful situations. I could feel that something stressful was on the horizon so I consciously began to put myself into a "control the stress" mindset that I had mastered during the time I worked as an agent.

Out on the street, the cops were sitting in an unmarked Ford in front of the house.

"I'll take my own car if you don't mind," I said.

"Sure," said Evans who was sitting on the passenger's side.

At the precinct I was taken into the captain's office with its small wooden desk, telephone, and four folding chairs. A few minutes later a beefy-faced white man in his sixties entered the room with Deke Robinson.

Deke had been an FBI agent, one of J. Edgar's boys. One of the very few black ones. He had taken early retirement to run for a seat in the state legislature and had won. It would be safe to say that his star was on the rise.

"Devil, thank you for coming," Deke said, shaking my hand. "I swear, I wouldn't have dragged you here unless it was an emergency. But you're the only person I know in Harlem who might be able to help us on this thing." He closed the door. "This is Captain Max Varney," Deke said, introducing the white man.

We acknowledged each other with hesitant nods.

Deke and I weren't chummy, but we'd never had any rude words between us either. He just wasn't my kind of person. To put it another way, I considered him a piece of shit.

Word on the street was that he took payoffs from drug dealers in return for arranging police protection, and Max Varney was his man on the inside. On the surface at least, Varney and Robinson were a study in contrasts. The policeman with his worn, shiny gabardine suit, plain shoes, and cheap aftershave; Deke with his manicured fingers, tailor-made suits, and brand new Mercedes. Deke was a smooth politician. His cool, dignified demeanor gained him the respect of the older folk, while his knowledge of the Harlem streets and his militant stance on civil rights issues made him popular with the young. When he took to the speaker's podium he had few rivals. Even Harlem's most fiery Baptist ministers had to admit that Deke Robinson could hold his own.

It wasn't smart to make an enemy of Deke Robinson unless you had to. Furthermore I was curious as to what shit he was cooking up. If Deke was involved, there was sure to be something stinky somewhere. And when the shit started to boil, and hit the fan, I wanted to be well out of range.

"To be honest, Dev," Deke continued, "I'm sitting on a powder keg, because there was a Japanese fellow killed up there in The Tease last night who turned out to be an important UN diplomat. A Katsu Yamaguchi."

"No shit."

He ignored my sarcasm and continued.

"As far as we can tell, he came up this way to buy himself a piece of ass and got wasted in the process."

"Black people get killed up here everyday and nobody gives a damn, so why bust a nut over some horny Jap, even if he was a diplomat?"

Deke sighed hard and gave me a look like his bowels were being twisted inside him.

The Captain simply glared.

"You know as well as I do, a diplomat getting iced up here can bring a lot of heat down on Harlem. We all got friends, families, and businesses that could get hurt."

"The Japanese," I said, "aren't they the same guys who fought against America in a big war a few years back? They sell you a few cars, stereos, and TVs, now you guys treat them like kings while black folk still get treated like yesterday's newspaper."

Deke continued.

"We need to catch the killers before this blows Harlem wide open. The NYPD have no leads and nobody else in Harlem has the know-how."

"Deke, honestly, I could give less than a shit. Let the Japs do their own legwork. Nobody led a special investigation when those kids killed my old man. Fuck 'em." I said

Deke sat in silence. Varney started to say something, but Deke cut him off with a stern look.

"Devil, I can't argue with you, but . . ." Deke paused. Then he began to explain what I already knew.

"The Republican Party in New York would love to hang every black Democratic politician out to dry, so that they can cut up Harlem among themselves and walk away with all the spoils. This Japanese diplomat thing could be their best excuse. Imagine what that would do to Harlem."

Deke was going for what he hoped was a soft spot. He hadn't gotten to be a state representative for nothing. His bullshit was twenty-four carat.

We had grown up only six blocks apart. Although he was older than me, we came from the same emotional background, shared the same culture, even some friends. But his brand of bullshit was all his own.

Politically, Harlem had always been a heavily Democratic district but with the last election the Republicans had gained control of the city, the state, and the Governor's office. Many black politicians who thought their Democratic futures had been ensured for life were now running for their political lives.

Deke elaborated further. "This diplomat represented some significant financial interests in Harlem, so if the shit really hits the fan it could open a Pandora's box that would not only hand the press and our enemies ammunition that could hurt us politically, but it could also have serious economic ramifications that could hurt a lot of important people personally. That's why certain people downtown don't want us to handle this investigation out in the open. They need the answers, but they need them in a quiet way. And I know you know how to find out things on the Q.T."

"Anything I can do in return to help you in any way, I'd be pleased to do," said the police Captain.

"Sorry gentleman, but I am not your man."

"Six dead bodies: two hookers, one diplomat, two Orientals, one coke dealer. Off the top of your head, just guesstimating, how would you read this thing?" Deke asked, fishing for clues.

"Six dead bodies in one apartment. I call that a mini-massacre. Just another bloodbath in Niggerville."

I knew that. And what's more, Deke knew that I knew. He was

going to have to deliver on this one. Otherwise his ass was in a sling along with Varney's.

I told him again, "I am not your man."

Varney flushed red, then a deep purple, then lost what little composure he was holding onto.

"Listen," he said as he advanced toward me. "You have a business here. Your friends have businesses too. They could be hurt a lot worse than you in this thing. If it's money that you're worried about, we'll pay all the expenses and take care of you too."

"Max!" Deke was trying to warn the Captain off.

"No, no Deke, I'll just say it flat out, so he'll understand. You say he's some kind of hot shot agent or something, you say he can find things out in Harlem that a police investigation never could, well he's gotta help us, simple as that. For your sake as well as mine."

"Max, just be cool," Deke warned him. "Be cool."

All the placating in the world would not have worked at that moment because Max Varney was a desperate man. He suddenly exploded, and the words began to pour from him like lava from Mt. St. Etna.

"I got two more years before retirement. I could lose my goddam pension and everything. I've put thirty fucking years into this department."

I looked at Varney and thought about something my grandmother used to say: "If you do right, right will follow you, and if you do wrong, the wrong you do will follow you too."

Max Varney was a man on the run from evil deeds and they were following close behind. He turned to me again.

"What about your uncle?" Varney asked.

"My uncle? What about him?"

"You know that he's running an illegal gambling joint not to mention he owns the club where this fiasco took place. The finger might be pointed directly at him if no conclusive answers are forthcoming . . . Christ Almighty, can't I get you people to understand that this business could bring the whole damn building crashing down on the guilty and innocent alike?"

Deke and I looked at each other. Then Deke icily stared Varney down. The police Captain wiped sweat from his brow then reached into his shirt pocket and pulled out a plastic packet that held pink tablets. Varney's racist reference to "you people" had not gone unnoticed. I didn't react. I didn't have to. I was the cat in this game and I had just uncovered a frightened mouse.

Deke, realizing Varney had gone too far, started backtracking.

"Listen, we all know Sultan's business is crooked. That's no secret," admitted Deke.

Varney downed the pink tablets without water.

"Goddamn ulcer," Varney complained.

"Get yourself some water and calm down." Deke bluntly told his partner in crime.

The Captain was in no mood to banter with Deke, this smooth talking Negro who looked like a cross between a movie star and a banker with his modern gold-rimmed eyeglasses and thousand-dollar European-cut suit. To make matters worse, a pain shot through Varney's gut that made him look like he wanted to cry.

"What I need is to find out who shot up that goddamn gook diplomat, okay?" said Varney. He sat down in one of the chairs, almost out of breath, and rubbed his eyes which had gone blood-shot from the strain of his outpouring.

"Come on Max, I'll finish this up by myself," Deke told the Captain as he opened the door to the office.

Varney gave me a dirty look and walked out. He was clearly more used to being the cat holding all the cards, bullying people to get what he wanted. Now, for a change, he knew how it felt to be the mouse. A mouse with an ulcer. The thought of it almost made me laugh out loud.

"I guess that's it then," I said, standing up to leave.

"I wish it was as simple as that," Deke said. The tone in his voice told me he had slipped off the velvet glove. I didn't know what angle the iron fist was coming from, but I was sure that I was about to find out.

Friday, 12:00 noon
■ Be-Bop Tavern

At the Be-Bop Tavern, Duke Rodgers, my head bartender, downed his third cup of coffee and winked at me. He was drawing my attention to the two elderly men sitting near the end of the bar. Goose Jones and Po Boy, regulars who show up religiously six mornings a week, drink until lunch, then return around three o'clock and stay until after the evening news. Both were retirees from the railroad and they'd been having the same arguments for as long as I'd known them, which was close to twenty years. People who had known them longer said that the arguments had been going on for at least thirty years.

Duke, who had flat feet, perched himself on a stool and started drying glasses. I acted like I was reading a magazine, but I was listening too.

"Man," said Goose with a slightly drunken slur, "I know my Bible, if I don't know nothing else. When Jesus comes back he's gonna be a Jew just like he was when he went up to heaven."

Po Boy was the son of a preacher. The fact that his father was the exalted Reverend Doctor Timothy F. Tweedle, a semi-illiterate, homespun Jack leg preacher who had enjoyed a bigger reputation for chasing the ladies than for delivering a good sermon, didn't affect his superior claim to biblical knowledge.

"He was a Christian when he went up to heaven," insisted Po Boy, "otherwise St. Peter wouldn't have allowed him through the pearly gates. Now, ain't no way he's gonna come back as nothing other than a one hundred percent pure Christian. Can you imagine all these Harlemite holy roller big-butt sistas washing the feet of some Jewish man with a funny little beanie cap on his head?"

Po Boy had a point. At least it made sense in the context of their Harlem logic. Goose took a long, hard swallow of beer to stimulate his brain for the next round of this intense debate.

"Tell me this," said Goose with an authoritative tone, "can a dog die as a dog and come back as a cat?"

Goose felt he had to break things down for his friend sometimes, because even though Po Boy had enjoyed more formal schooling than himself, he wasn't so quick on the uptake about things that demanded deep thought, like religion and gambling.

"That's blasphemy. How you gonna go and call Jesus a dog?" Po Boy shot back.

"I didn't call Jesus no dog," Goose replied. "Man you drunk."

"Hey bossman," called Goose over his shoulder to where I was standing. "Bossman, tell this Negro, if Jesus died a Jew wouldn't he have to come back a Jew?"

"My name is Wess and I ain't in this mess," I called back. "Besides I hadn't been paying attention, I was reading," I grinned over at Duke, who was shaking his head in amazement.

Duke laughed out loud at my lie and moved off his perch to serve a customer who had just walked in. Christine, my evening manager, had come in early and was cleaning off the tables in the row of booths by the wall, getting them ready for the afternoon rush. She was nearly thirty but looked closer to forty. Even though she watched her diet, did regular exercise, and went to church at least one Sunday in each month, Christine hadn't had much luck with men. Her last boyfriend, Samson, had run off with someone else when she was three months pregnant. Hadn't even offered to help her pay for the abortion. Still, she wasn't the kind to cry over spilt milk. She was just grateful that she had found a steady job to help her raise the two children she already had.

"Hey baby, I feel lucky this week," Duke called over to Christine. "If I hit the numbers, I'll take you to Atlantic City. Let you knock yourself out."

"You better stop flirting with me, old man, before I make you live up to your promises," Christine teased.

I was in the back, checking on the new beer pumps when Christine informed me that a pretty lady was out front waiting to see

me. The pretty lady was my cousin, Katherine Johnson. We hugged
and kissed, our usual greeting.

Kit Kat, or just Kit, probably knew me better than anyone else.
We had always been close. This was the first time she had come by
the bar since my father's death. Like me, she was haunted by his
memory.

We sat down in a booth near the back of the bar. I told Duke to
bring a coke for me and hot chocolate for her.

"What kind of wind blew you in here?" I asked.

"Checking you out," she smiled looking around at the bar. "It
looks just the same."

"That's because it is the same. Only difference is, I run it now."

"Just don't run it into the ground, okay," she teased. "Listen,
have you gotten yourself hooked up with any ladies yet, because
I've got a friend who would like to meet you ?"

"No, not yet."

"I bet you're knockin' boots with some skeezer with a set of big
you-know-whats in the front and a big you-know-what in the
back, ain't you? Come on 'fess up, I know you, Dev: Bim Bam,
thank you ma'am, see you next time when I can, right? You still
seeing Maxine I bet, ain't you ?"

All I could do was laugh. That had been my M.O. for many
years and she had all of my moves down pat.

"When are you going to settle down?"

"When, are *you* going to settle down?" The words flew out of
my mouth and hovered in midair. Our eyes met. There was an
awkward moment of silence and, almost at the same instant, we
burst out laughing together.

"Well at least it wasn't all bad," I joked. "Horace did help you
get interested in Law."

"And he also helped me study for and pass that damn bar
exam," she added. "Shoot, after I spent all that time studying and
sweating for that piece of paper, he could have had an affair with
a giraffe and I wouldn't have cared."

I admired my cousin, she was a trooper. Her marriage to Horace, a brilliant attorney, had broken up after she caught him in

bed with someone else. Another man. But she had gotten over it quickly and was now seeing another lawyer who was also brilliant and made even more money than Horace. His name was Larry, I think. I had met him once or twice. Talked football and stuff but didn't have much personality. Kit had been taught from the cradle that Harlem was full of good-looking men with personality. Men so broke they couldn't buy a piece of penny candy, but full of personality. Since Larry was successful and had money, I'm sure Kit's thinking was that she possessed enough personality for the both of them.

"How's Uncle Beans?" I asked.

People who knew him for business purposes called him Sultan or Mr. Johnson. But the old-timers who knew him as a tough, mouthy kid growing up in the streets of Harlem in the old days, and those few people who were really close to him, called him Beans. That's all my father and mother or Aunt Velma ever called him.

"He's all right," she said. "Complaining sometimes about his stomach, that's all."

"Has he seen a doctor?"

"Now you know the answer to that," she laughed. "The doctor and the tax man are two people Daddy could go without ever seeing."

"I know that's right." I laughed.

Then we laughed some more. It felt good talking to someone with whom I could be myself. We sipped our drinks for a while without saying anything, comfortable enough so that neither one of us needed to fill the silence. After a while she said that she had had a call from Deke Robinson earlier that morning and that he had invited her to breakfast.

"What did he want?" I asked knowing what the answer would most likely be.

"He talked about what happened at The Tease, and wanted to know if there was any way I could get you to help find out who killed the Japanese guy up there and why."

"What did you say?"

She grinned deviously. "I told him that black sexual exoticism was world famous and that the diplomat was most probably just looking to get his little taste."

"You're lucky. As slimy as Deke is, I'm surprised he didn't try to use that as an opening to proposition you on the spot."

"No, but what he did do was sneakily let it drop that he knows I'm trying to get a job at the DA's office, and that my helping him out would give him a reason to help me out."

"What a skunk. Did he go so far as to say that if you didn't help him he would do all he could to block your application?"

"Not in so many words, but the implication was definitely there," she said.

"Have you mentioned it to Uncle Beans yet?"

"Not yet, I wanted to run it past you first. Deke said he talked with you on the subject last night."

"He did and I turned him down flat. He's under heavy political pressure to come up with some answers."

"I knew there was more to it than he was saying."

"With Deke Robinson there always is. Let me think how to best approach this. I'll work something out, don't worry."

"Speaking of girl friends, have you heard the latest?"

"Tell me."

"Well," she paused to keep me in suspense then said, "Daddy's in love, chile."

"What . . . ?

"L.O.V.E." Kit said.

"Who?" I asked astonished.

"Barbara Simmons. Some lady he met at one of those art gallery things he goes to, and she hit on him. The sparks are really flying." Kit smiled.

"You met her yet?"

"Yeah, she seems all right. She lets him boss her around and she treats him just like a baby. You know he goes for all that Tarzan of the Jungle stuff, like all you men do."

"Like old folks go for soft shoes." I agreed.

"Daddy is sixty-seven now. I guess he figures he needs someone to grow old with."

"Maybe. I guess time changes everything, and everybody," I philosophized.

"As long as she makes him happy." Kit smiled. "That's what I say. You know he has had a lot of women since Momma died, but he hasn't ever taken anybody too seriously."

"How long has it been now?"

"Twelve years this coming December."

I had been in Europe and not planning to make it home for Christmas when I got a call from my Dad saying that my Aunt Velma wasn't expected to last much longer. The cancer she had fought for so long had finally beaten her. I changed all my plans and came home from Europe for the funeral. I was one of her pallbearers.

"All we can say is God bless him, and let's hope she can make the old boy happy."

Kit agreed.

We continued talking for more than an hour, about people we had grown up with and what they were doing now and also about plans we each had for the future. She talked about her hopes of joining the D.A.'s staff and I told her how I intended to remodel the bar.

After she left I went back to working on how to fix the refrigeration system. I spent almost a half-hour looking through the files to find the original purchase receipt or the warranty card. For some reason thoughts of Amanda kept flying into my head but I fought to ignore them. Well, as much as I could anyway. As I continued working I also thought about Deke Robinson and his conversation with my cousin Kit. Deke had taken the velvet glove off the iron fist. Now he had thrown his first punch.

The wind was blowing icicle cold in great, hard gusts from the west as I rounded the corner at 125th Street and Adam Clayton Powell. I entered the State Office Building located in the same block a few minutes later.

"It cold as a witches titty, ain't it?" the elderly guard laughed as I blew warm breath onto my hands and winced as the sound of the freezing wind blew past the doorway into the building.

I took an elevator up to the eighth floor. In a corner of the north wing a mahogany door bore the name J. Johnson Enterprises. I rang the bell and waited until the receptionist asked me to identify myself. The buzzer sounded to let me inside.

"Miss Pritchard asked me to take you through." The receptionist was in her early twenties, with a light tan complexion and a pleasant smile. She had short black hair, cut into a pageboy with blond streaks near the front.

I followed her into another section of the office. Miss Pritchard greeted me as I rounded the corner.

"Marcus, how have you been?"

Miss Pritchard was a rare gem. She had been my uncle's secretary and confidante for over twenty-five years. At every birthday, and on every special occasion, she had always been there. She was the family friend, always there to help. Her smile radiated something warm and wonderful from a kind face I had known a long time. Her lithe, trim figure always looked the same: neat, efficient, hair pulled back in a bun, glasses, the same even temperament, pleasant with a certain business-like and personable grace. She never pried into other people's affairs and never offered any advice she wasn't asked for. I'd never heard anyone say anything negative about Miss Pritchard.

Her small portable radio which was always tuned to the classical music frequency was kept at a volume so low it was barely audible. She was the picture of dignity and loyalty. Dad had always referred to her as Miss Pritchard and she had referred to him as Mr. Barnett. As a teenager I often suspected there was something more between them, but neither of them was the type to kiss and tell. At the cemetery, on the day of Dad's funeral, after he had been buried and as the last of the funeral cars were leaving, I remember her still standing by the gravesite crying softly.

Miss Pritchard hugged me in a way that let me know that we both shared a loss that was beyond words.

"Your mother would have been so proud to see you such a successful young man," she said smiling.

"Thank you."

"Your uncle is waiting for you."

Uncle Beans sat at his large maple desk looking at a computer print out.

"How you doing?" he asked, peeping over the top of his reading glasses.

My uncle was neatly muscled, stood about five eight, and weighed about one hundred and sixty pounds soaking wet. In short he was fit and looked it except for a small gut protruding from his middle. His thinning salt-and-pepper hair was permanently and naturally waved, a result of wearing it brushed straight back and sleeping in a stocking cap for most of his life. He smoked Cuban cigars, wore a large emerald ring on his left hand, and a diamond studded Rolex on his wrist. Today he was dressed in a made-to-measure, tan double-breasted pinstriped suit, a style that had become his trademark over the past forty years.

"Okay, how about you?"

He shrugged.

"You know."

I did. I plopped down in a large leather seat opposite him. He looked across the desk and waited for me to speak. From the way he was smiling I knew he was probably already aware of what I was about to say. His grapevine was phenomenal.

I told him about Kit's meeting with Deke. He just nodded coolly and swiveled his chair around and peered out of the window without speaking. He then picked up the phone and dialed a number. He pressed the speakerphone button on his telephone and winked at me. After a few seconds, Varney's voice came on the line.

"Listen, you simple-minded fuck," Uncle Beans began, "what the hell you doing getting Deke Robinson to put pressure on my daughter? Police or no police, I'll have your ass up on racketeering charges. Think I don't know the right people? I'll have internal affairs up your ass so far up shit creek, you'll need an ocean liner to tow it out."

"B-b-but . . ." Varney tried to get a word in edgewise, but Uncle Beans cut him off. He was on a roll.

"Listen Varney, I don't want to hear shit, you're the law, you're supposed to solve murders. And if you couldn't why didn't you call me first? It's my damn place. What the fuck Deke Robinson got to do with it anyway?"

"B-b-but . . . I just thought . . ." the police captain tried again, but my uncle cut him off once more. I pictured Varney going for his pink ulcer tablets again.

"Listen, if you ever try and squeeze my family again, you bastard, you'll be sorry for the rest of your miserable fucking life."

"I'm sorry, uh" said Varney, like he didn't know whether to shit or go blind.

"Listen, I will get back to you on this later."

Uncle Beans slammed the phone down, then looked over at me and smiled like the cat that had just swallowed the canary.

"Well, I got him nervous," he smiled calmly, "at least for now."

One of the lessons I had learned long ago from Dad and Uncle Beans was that when you were faced with a problem, the most important rule was never to panic. They had taught me to think my way out and then choose my plan of action. But never let emotion rule. Even when you let the other person think you are reacting to emotion, in your own head you have to remain as cool as a cucumber.

"How much damage can Deke really do?" I wanted to know.

"Probably more than I'd like to admit, he could screw up

Katherine's career. You see," Uncle Beans explained, "Deke will spread some shit on Katherine and sell her down the river. Then he'll leak it to some Republican news reporter who will write a story raising questions about Katherine being the daughter of a Harlem kingmaker. As a result, the Republicans will put one of their own people in that DA spot. Deke's payoff from the Republicans will be that they will then owe him a favor. I can spread some money around, which will neutralize things. But that is going to take a few weeks. In the meantime, Katherine could get knocked out of the box. And to be honest, I would rather not have that. If you could find out what really happened at The Tease the other night, it would really be useful, get me?"

"Gotcha. I'll think about it and let you know late tonight."

"Okay." He nodded. "I'll be here."

It was a heavy decision that we both knew needed some time and space. I stood up to leave.

"By the way, congratulations."

"On what?" A puzzled look appeared across his dark brown features.

"On falling in love." Despite my efforts a smile broke through my straight face.

"Ah shit," he grinned embarrassed that I had caught him off guard. "Man you crazy, you know I'm too old for that kinda stuff." He smiled sheepishly then picked up the newspaper from his desk and playfully threw it at me. He was still grinning as I left the office.

I had decided not to drive because I needed to travel into Midtown. I had ordered some old jazz tunes from a specialty store called Colony Records and traveling there by subway was more efficient, plus it cost less. The cheapest parking would set me back at least ten bucks. For guys who were making big money, ten bucks was nothing, but for me ten bucks was still the cost of a meal. I hopped the A train at Lenox Avenue and rode down to 59th Street. Colony Records was on 49th and Seventh, but I needed time to think so I decided to walk the ten blocks. As I walked, I thought about the problem facing me and the players involved.

The world was not painted in black and white, right and wrong, good and bad. Though we as humans oftentimes seek to make the world less complicated and safer by dividing it into simple categories — placing the answers to life's problems neatly into a box of one sort or the other — the truth was that we all lived somewhere within the many shades of gray that life created around us. Shades of reality. When it all boiled down, what made Uncle Beans different from any other businessman running a major corporation? True, he ran illegal gambling operations. True, part of his living derived from breaking the law, but so did a lot of peoples'. That said, every politician or legitimate businessman would likely have been proven guilty in a court of law for influence peddling. And all in the name of freedom and democracy. The difference was, Uncle Beans didn't have laws or a bureaucracy or a powerful political party to hide behind now. He just had his street smarts. He was what he was and never made any apology for it. He wasn't an angel, but he never pretended to be. And then again neither was I. During my time as a CIA operative I had knowingly participated in illegal activities for the government. Illegal activities sanctioned by the highest offices in the land. Sometimes it would be in the name of decency, sometimes in the name of God and country, or of survival. I guess when I hit the glass ceiling, which was about the same time Dad died, I started asking myself a few questions.

Questions like, was it more justifiable for me to murder a man whom I had never met, who had never done anything to me, simply because some asshole boss told me that he was an enemy of the state? I guess it was thoughts like these that led me to leave the CIA. Anyway, Varney was scrambling for his job. Deke was scrambling to get a bigger toehold in a corrupt political system so that he could become even more corrupt.

The corrupt downtown big shots were up in arms because some Japanese diplomat had taken a bullet. On every side of this three-sided deal nobody's hands were clean. I just had to determine which side of the deal I wanted to stand on. Point blank, if there had to be a sacrificial lamb, it would be Uncle Beans. One reason was that Uncle Beans was the king of the shadow politicians in Harlem, which is a very important political role. Shadow politicians don't get elected to political offices, but rather pull the strings of those who do. Over the years, the men in the shadows became so powerful they effectively operated as the agents for downtown moneymen who knew that Harlem was valuable but didn't have the access that would enable them to reap the benefits.

Using their access to money and influence the shadow politicians were able to get men elected to local public office for the Democratic party, men that people knew nothing about except at election time when their faces showed up on posters. From his shadow position over the past thirty years Uncle Beans had acquired power throughout Harlem. At least that had been the case until now. Now, all the friends and contacts loyal to the Democratic party he had done business with over the past thirty years were reeling from the vengeance of a major political upset that brought in a new Republican regime. And Uncle Beans was a big Democratic fish that the Republican newspapers would love to vilify for the killings at his club. If I didn't make a move to help then without a doubt Uncle Beans would be scrambling to keep what had taken him thirty years to build, including Kit's chance of a great legal career.

I knew that the powers that be had demanded blood for the killing of this diplomat. And at this stage of the game, I knew that anybody's blood would do

My main concern was that it should not become the blood of the people I loved. Uncle Beans was being very cool about the whole thing, which meant he was really very nervous. If it had just been a killing, any killing in the Tease Me Club, all the excitement would have blown over in a couple days and things would have returned to normal. But this was different. A diplomat was involved. Nobody wanted a scandal involving a Japanese diplomat, least of all certain big shot Democratic politicians downtown whose names might be linked with some shady deals Yamaguchi had going in Harlem.

I
t was almost ten when I rang my uncle's office. He answered
the phone.

"I'm in," I said.

"Good." Uncle Beans sounded pleased, as I knew he would.

I explained that I needed to get a few things together which I'd
do that evening and, after that, I'd go see Varney. I also asked if he
would call ahead and get Varney to arrange for me to see the bodies of those who had lost their lives in the rooms above the Tease
Me Club on that eventful night.

He said he would and thanked me again.

"Listen," I said, "I've got a favor to ask."

"Name it."

"That first boy child you get, name it after me, okay?"

Uncle Beans let out a loud laugh.

I had been out all day and my stomach was talking to me. I
grabbed a gypsy cab and rode to 145th near the corner of Broadway. I walked halfway down the block and turned into a doorway
with a red, green, and yellow hand-painted sign on the front window that read "Walter Dixon's Soul Food Heaven." I ordered a feast.
There were oxtails, hot spiced chicken, macaroni and cheese, but-
terbeans, and cornbread. Walter, the owner, walked over and
watched me devouring his food.

"Look like you hungry, man," he said in an accent that hadn't
changed since his days as a Georgia farm boy.

"Hungry ain't the word," I returned and kept eating.

"Enjoy it then," he said and moved off to check on his other
customers.

"Hey, Mister High-an'-Mighty Barnett, how come you haven't
called me like you said you would?"

I turned in the direction of the voice I knew only too well.

It belonged to Sheila Masters. She sat opposite me as I went on eating.

"Have some," I offered.

"So you'd rather eat Walter's cooking than mine?" she asked directly.

"No, I haven't called you because I've been busy with plans to remodel my place," I lied.

I allowed my eyes to meet hers. Sheila was one of those beautiful women that made you want her the moment you saw her. Model material. She had beautiful skin, a beautiful body, the works. Except when you got to know her, it didn't matter. She more than made up for her beauty by being a royal pain in the ass.

"I'm giving a party at my place next week. Come, and bring some friends."

"Sure, give me the date." Even though I had no intention of going, it was better to come up with an excuse later than to object now.

"And bring something to drink too," she added.

"Okay, whatever," I said.

I had made the serious mistake of having an affair with Sheila. A few months back Sheila had come into the bar with someone I knew, and we had been attracted to each other. One thing had led to another and we ended up in the bedroom. After that Sheila had called me every day, sometimes four or five times a day, wanting to do this and that, or to tell me that she had just broken a nail or put a run in her stocking. I was convinced that Sheila was one step from being certifiable. In addition to being nutty, Sheila was jealous, and possessive, but I had asked her to meet me at Walter's because I needed to get in touch with the woman with whom she had come into my bar that first time, Celeste Miller. Celeste was the sister of a guy I needed to contact for the job I was about to do. The problem was, I couldn't ask Sheila directly for Celeste's number because Sheila would assume I wanted to hit on her friend. I didn't have a plan other than just to play it by ear.

We talked about Sheila's dance class, her job at the nursery school, her grandmother's hip operation, her opinion on celibacy for women of higher consciousness, her microbiotic diet plan. Then we talked about Sheila's plans for going away to the Zen temple during the Christmas holidays. Get the picture? Sheila made Glenn Close in *Fatal Attraction* seem like Shirley Temple.

As she talked on and on and on about what she thought of the latest Eddie Murphy movie, I was having a fantasy of tying Sheila to the chair right there in the restaurant and pouring hot sauce down her throat until she gave me the number, when a miracle happened. Wayne Salters walked into the restaurant. Wayne is one of my regular customers at the bar. We get along. He saw me and waved a greeting. I called him over and introduced him to Sheila as a very good friend of mine. Steered the conversation around to the fact that Wayne used to play pro-ball for the Atlanta Hawks which I knew would get Sheila's attention. As we spoke I turned towards Wayne, so that Sheila couldn't see my face and winked to him to play along. Wayne is a smart guy and he did. I mentioned that I had won some tickets for a ski resort and that it would be great for him to come along except he had just broken up with his girlfriend. Then I suggested Celeste because he was just her type. Without hesitation Sheila wrote down the digits. I committed them to memory as she pressed Wayne to call Celeste that night before it was too late.

Later that night, I called Celeste. She answered on the second ring. I explained about Sheila and how and why I got her number. She said she understood and told me that I had her sympathy. In fact, she said, anyone who had ever dated Sheila had her sympathy. We laughed. She gave me the number I needed, I thanked her and hung up.

I took out a notepad and wrote down a few things. At the top of the list was the name I had just gotten, that of Celeste's brother, Randy. A few years back, when the CIA was investigating an international heroin ring operating between Amsterdam and New York, Randy Miller had offered his services as a snitch. He was smart and in addition he was an expert at playing both ends against the middle. I rang him and set up a meeting for the following night. I didn't have the exact time, but I told him to wait for my call.

The night evaporated with the soft sounds of George Benson's guitar lulling me to sleep, and morning rushed in with the sound of my alarm and the weather forecast.

I bathed and did my morning ritual of exercises that included a battery of sit-ups, push-ups, and yoga positions. My body was still in good shape. I weighed 160 pounds and stood six foot even. I boxed two nights a week at the Y on 135th Street and still played basketball with guys half my age. Still, I had to be careful. Sickle cell is a condition that affects the hemoglobin. The disease cuts off the supply of oxygen from the red blood cells, causing them to develop into a sickle shape, clogging up in the veins, and stopping the flow of blood to the rest of the body. The result is extreme pain and if not checked can easily result in death. Many sickle cell carriers die in childhood and most I know have spent a major portion of their lives in and out of hospitals, even to the point where it has totally disrupted their lives. But I have been extremely lucky. My crisis attacks have been few and far between and I can live a pretty normal life if I maintain certain diet and exercise routines. Still, an attack could come on at any time for any number of reasons.

I put on my casual green khaki trousers with a thick brown pullover and a brown bomber jacket and headed for the precinct. Varney met me with a handshake. His buddy Deke was nowhere to be seen. I went into his office and he closed the door.

"I'm sorry if we had any misunderstanding the other day," he forced a smile. He informed me that he had made the necessary calls to the morgue that I had requested through my uncle. Then he handed me an envelope containing a copy of the police reports taken at the scene of the crime. I read them quickly and made a couple notes.

At 10:46 A.M. I arrived at the morgue and was told by an olive-skinned woman with short brown and orange hair that Dr. Polonski was expecting me. I followed her and three corridors later arrived at the office of the Director of Criminal Pathology. Polonski received me with a firm handshake. He was a short, round man who walked with a slight limp. As we made our way along the corridor to see the bodies, he explained that they had already done autopsies on them. The six bodies were lined up against a wall on stainless steel tables. The walls were a sickly off-white color and the floor was white tiled with drainage ditches alongside the tables.

He handed me the autopsy reports and talked about the forensic cause of death for each corpse. Four of the corpses were routine cases. It was the other two I found interesting. The years of training came back to me as I examined the angle and point of entry of the fatal wound in the fat Asian's body.

"We counted seventy-three knife wounds on this one," the pathologist explained. "Incredible. You wouldn't believe it, but we get about six of these multiple stab victims per month. You wouldn't believe human beings would act like that."

"Yes, I would." I said matter of factly.

I didn't tell Polonski that one of the nicest and most charming guys I had ever met was Solomon Morgenstern. Morgenstern was probably also the most heartless assassin I'd ever met. He'd lived in the Treblinka Concentration Camp from the age of six to nine. He'd seen so much death and killing that terrible acts of violence had become normal and perfectly acceptable. He wasn't what one would consider a casebook sociopath or a sadist either, but rather a person whose perception of morality had been altered by his environment. Though I hadn't articulated it, I knew it was that part of myself that I shared with Solomon Morgenstern that I now wanted to hide from the world. More importantly, to hide from myself.

"Says here both Asian victims were killed with a blade that had a serrated edge."

"Yeah," the doctor confirmed.

I examined more closely the soles of the big Asian's feet and requested the use of a scalpel. The doctor handed me one with a look of interest. I ran it along the outer soles of the dead men's feet.

"Thanks," I said handing back the scalpel.

The doctor looked and waited without saying a word.

"Both these Asians got a lot of calluses on their feet, huh," I said.

"Looks like it," Polonski said flatly.

I thanked Dr. Polonski and left. I headed back up the FDR towards Harlem listening to the sounds of Sarah Vaughn. My trip to the morgue had unearthed two important things. One, that the Asians' callused feet suggested that they probably were martial arts assassins; two, what I had not told the doctor was that the man who killed both Asian assassins had himself been a trained assassin. Sometimes it takes one to know one.

Saturday, 6:00 P.M.
■ A Rented Room Somewhere in Harlem

*T*he man with the dead eyes had not slept for two days and two nights. Following the bloody jubilation, energy had been pounding ceaselessly in his brain. The constant buzzing in his head made him want to cry out with both pain and ecstasy simultaneously. It kept him from sleep. Thoughts tumbled randomly about in his brain like clothes in a spin dryer. The dried blood of the big Asian man that had splattered on his face and hands was still evident. This dried blood was now three days old. A scar on his face still throbbed despite the applied antiseptic. His mind ached. He could hear the sound of a baby screaming loudly and wolves howling. His mind was a battlefield of enemies from the past who rose up to invade his consciousness.

He was waiting for her, his very own angel. She was sometimes late. He didn't like her being late, but it was all right. He could withstand any pain because he loved her. Loved her voice purring deep into his ear. It cleansed his filthy and cluttered mind. Her mouth on his body. She was his sweet angel. He waited for her and let his mind drift back to another time, a time when things were new, before the green jungle, before the napalm, before the blood, before the pain. Before the baking of the brain inside his skull.

He could hear the screams again and felt blood splashing his face. Somebody was talking in a voice he knew. It was a man's voice. It mixed in with his blood-soaked thoughts.

"My meat got so hard last night, I dreamed I screwed a gorilla," the voice screamed.

Then suddenly there were sounds of laughter all around. And the man with the dead eyes was laughing too. The man with the dead eyes could hear the old man and woman in the apartment next door talking through the wall.

They were eating dinner and discussing him.

"That man sounds like he's dying over there in that room," Mrs. Ida Jenkins said to her husband Mr. Willie.

"Yeah maybe," Mr. Willie replied.

"Don't you eat up all those black-eyed peas Willie, we got to eat tomorrow too. And stop loading them peas up with so much hot sauce, you gon' be up going to the bathroom all night and I won't get one minute's sleep." The woman told her husband.

The man with the dead eyes could hear them talking as clearly as if he had been sitting there at the dinner table with them, shoving peas into his own mouth.

"Maybe we should go see about him, maybe he's sick, maybe he wants something to eat," the lady said.

"I done told you before, Ida, to keep your darn nose out of other folks' business. He may have that woman over there. He's a single man after all."

"You talking crazy," lda insisted. "What kind of man would scream like that when he was carrying on with a woman?"

"He get the right one over there, I'll be damn if she don't make him crow like a young rooster." This time there was laughter in the old man's voice.

"Instead of thinking such nasty thoughts, Willie Jenkins, you should be thinking about your bible lesson for tomorrow," Ida reprimanded.

The man with the dead eyes could still hear them talking. But now he wanted to stop listening and start walking. He wanted to walk for a while.

He began to pace back and forth inside his room. Back and forth like a mad tiger in a cage. Back and forth. He would pace until his angel came. She always came, and when she did she would bring him sanity.

He walked for miles inside that room. Waiting for his angel.

The man with dead eyes had been born a long time ago to a nineteen-year-old prostitute working in a Kansas whorehouse for a lady called Tessy. When he was twelve years old his mother married Big Sam, who was in the army.

   Soon after, two men in a truck drove up and told his mother Big
Sam was dead. A few weeks later, his mother told him she was going
to the store and left him in Big Sam's house with ten dollars. She
never came back, never wrote. Nothing. Never.
   A man from the state took the boy with dead eyes and put him
into an orphanage where he lived until he joined the army on the
day he turned seventeen.
   Presently the man with dead eyes got tired and lay down on the
floor. He was on the floor when she knocked on the door. He opened
it and she walked in. Heaven opened up and he almost smiled. His
angel gave him the magic elixir of love that quieted the screaming
inside his head. Then he went to sleep. Hours later when he woke she
had stripped him naked and washed away the blood. She was still
there, his angel, and she was naked too. She made love to him and
spoke sweet-nothings in her angelic voice. He belonged to her.

I pulled off the Van Wyck Expressway onto the Union Turnpike exit, drove about a quarter of a mile then made a right at Parsons Blvd. and drove another ten minutes until I reached Jamaica Avenue, which was the street where Melvin Hodges lived. As I walked towards the address he'd given me on the phone, Melvin opened the door.

"Find it all right?" he asked me.

"Yeah, no sweat."

He offered me coffee. I drank two cups as we looked through a large box of photographs of go-go dancers that he kept neatly catalogued and meticulously arranged. They dated back to June 1968. Most of them had been taken in the Tease Me Club with the girls wearing their stage dance costumes. There were over five hundred of them. Melvin said he kept a file on each girl just in case one ever made it to the big-time. He'd already sold three photos to a scandal magazine for a nice piece of change.

But that was just one side of it. The more practical side was that Melvin had kept a photograph, biography, and signature on each girl who had danced at the Tease Me Club because people would sometimes come around needing information about them. And information meant money. On several occasions someone had turned up looking for one of the girls, loaded down with a pocket full of money and looking to get married. A couple times it had been the cops, looking for one who had passed bad checks or ran a scam of sorts.

In any case, it always spelled money. Uncle Beans and Melvin had a 60/40 split going on the deal. On a few occasions, this box of photographs had paid off big. I was hoping that this would be one of them.

"I don't think she ever danced for us, she's just a kid. Just starting to hang out. You know the type, twenty-two going on forty-five," Melvin told me, adjusting the glasses that always seem to slide forward on his nose.

He was right, I did know the type.

"But I do remember a girl named Inez who danced for us, who she was tight with, yeah." A light bulb seemed to have lit up inside Melvin's head. "This kid, I remember her good now, she used to hang out around Inez a lot. Wanted to be like Inez. Yeah that's the one, I know that for a fact."

We were talking about a girl he had seen going up to China Blue's party, a youngish girl he had not told the police about, a girl who had not turned up dead. Her street name was Peter Pan. Where was she now? Melvin made a few calls and came up with a place to reach Inez Fuentes. It directed me to Spanish Harlem.

What had once been principally an Italian district of the city on the east side near 116th and First Avenue had more recently become filled with immigrants from places like Santo Domingo, Peru, Mexico, and Honduras. All the stores on the block had signs in Spanish. Cuchifrito stands, tropical vegetable stands, and Latino travel agencies covered the entire block. You name it, 116th had it. Most of the Italians who still lived there were senior citizens who had been there all their lives and were not about to leave no matter how many cuchifrito stands popped up. Some of these senior citizens were the parents of Mafia types, consequently one could walk the streets without the fear of being robbed . . . at least not in broad daylight.

The place I was looking for stood right on the corner facing west at First Avenue. The red brick building sported a large billboard on its north side advertising the virtues of Camel cigarettes in Spanish. I looked at my watch. It was still early, only 12:30 P.M. I sat in a diner across the street, drank an over-priced orange juice from a can, and read the sports section of the Sunday *New York Times* while Latino families dressed in bright colors returned from the various Catholic churches in the neighborhood. When it got to be 1:00 P.M., I walked across the street and rang the bell. The Latino guy who opened the door looked about thirty-five. He had a face like a bulldog and looked as if he had been seriously overdosing on Hostess Twinkies and beans and rice. He stood about five six and his belly stuck out about six inches beyond his pants. A real butterball.

"Yeah?" he said glowering at me. "What you want?"

"I'm looking for Inez. I'm a friend of Melvin's from the Tease Me Club."

The butterball's faced acquired a nasty scowl.

"Hold on," he muttered and slammed the door in my face.

He came back a minute later.

"She don't know no Melvin," he spat contemptuously.

"She just spoke to him on the phone this morning. She told me to come by." I insisted.

He looked puzzled and then decided that he didn't want to be bothered.

"Well, she say she don't know you."

Just then Inez's high-pitched nasal-tinged voice rang out from behind the butterball.

"Oh yeah, yeah, I remember now. I was asleep." Her face appeared over his shoulder. "Yeah, Mel. Tall Mel with glasses, right?" she said. "The bartender at The Tease, sure I know him, that's my friend. Come in."

The butterball relented and opened the door. I stepped into the house. The place was a mess. Inez closed the door behind me.

"This is my husband, Roberto," she whined, introducing the butterball.

From outward appearances, Inez Fuentes didn't seem to have much going for herself in the husband department, or the brains department, but the way she looked it wouldn't have mattered if she had carried her brain in a cardboard box. She was drop-dead gorgeous. Even without makeup she was a knockout. She was about twenty-five and had the face of a beauty queen and a body that would make a blind man see. She wore a flimsy nylon see-through bathrobe with only panties and a bra underneath.

"Sit down," she said, clearing off an eight-inch square on the couch. "What's your name?"

"Barnett."

I sat down and the butterball took what must have been his usual seat in a reclining chair in front of the wide screen TV. He was watching Ren and Stimpy. I told her who I was trying to find.

"Nooo, I ain't seen her for a long time, about almost a month," Inez told me in her nasal tone.

"Do you know her real name?"

"Ah, her first name is, ah . . . let me think, Donna. I ain't sure though."

"Did she have a boyfriend?"

Butterball was pretending to check out the TV, but taking in every word that was being said. I could tell Inez didn't feel comfortable. I shifted a quick glance in her direction and she picked up the signal.

"Roberto," she asked, "go get my cigarettes in the room please."

"You get 'em," he said without looking up.

"I am talking, would you please get my cigarettes, damn."

Her voice took on an edge and Roberto jumped his fat ass up and went to get the smokes. He may have been the man, but it was obvious that she wore the pants. The second he was out of the room, I slipped her a rolled up hundred-dollar bill I had prepared beforehand.

Money talks and bullshit walks. Ten minutes later I was walking back towards my car. The money had suddenly brought a lot of facts flashing back into Inez's cloudy memory. Peter Pan's real name was Donna Flowers. Donna sold weed sometimes for her boyfriend Yuseff, who drove a 4x4, and could usually be found hanging out in Marcus Garvey Park on 120th between Lenox and Fifth Avenue playing basketball. Inez didn't have Donna's number, or address, but had a friend who would probably have it because she sometimes bought weed from Donna.

The friend was a hooker named Marta who worked out of a bar on 113th and Second Avenue. Marta would be there later tonight, after 10:00 P.M. She wrote a note in Spanish on a ragged piece of paper that would let Marta know I was kosher.

I still had not gotten a real fix on anything that took me a step closer to the answers I needed, but now at least I had a little something. And at this stage a little something was better than a whole lot of nothing.

I made a few more scribbles in my notebook and headed uptown towards Marcus Garvey Park. There were about fifteen guys on the basketball court in the park. Although it was chilly some of them had no shirts on. They were sweating stylishly and playing their hearts out. The men ranged in age from late teens to early forties. Some of the players were making the kinds of funky moves that I had only witnessed a few times before and then only on TV.

Basketball is part of the African American phenomenon. And as I watched them playing I began to think about all of the thousands of excellent young black ball players throughout America whose hoop dreams were of cracking the NBA. Hoping and praying that maybe, just maybe, they would be the next Michael Jordan. Few probably considered themselves as the next million-dollar computer genius or Wall Streeter. But buying into the hype of million dollar hoop dreams was a lot easier than buying into the hard cold reality of a low paying job, the constant shadow of racism, and a grinding week to week existence.

The hype was loaded in favor of ball players, entertainers, and big-time drug dealers. While growing up in Harlem, several of my friends like Pete Coleman, Hershell Wendell, Nestor Ruiz, and Jenette Bennet had all bought into the hype offered by the street life of fast money and neighborhood fame. Unfortunately, most of them were dead now.

I asked around about Yuseff.

"Yuseff, drive a 4x4, chat-a-lotta shit, right?" one of the players said. He had a slight build, chocolate skin, orange Nike running shoes, and a West Indian accent.

"Yeah that's him," I said.

"Stick around, him soon come. You wanna cop? I got the bomb sess."

"No, I'm cool. Thanks." I was not in the market to buy weed.

In the West Indian culture, "soon come" might mean five minutes, five hours, or it could even mean five days, depending on who says it. But I waited, and after two hours Yuseff did come.

Yuseff was in his mid-to-late twenties, about two inches taller than me, and had a muscular build. A tattoo between his right thumb and forefinger identified him as a gangbanger who had served time, which explained the muscles. Pumping iron was a popular way of passing time in the joint.

Yuseff strutted onto the court, waited around for a spot to open, then began playing. He played two games, then took a break.

I approached Yuseff quietly, identifying myself as a friend of someone looking to get in touch with Donna Flowers. I told him she might be in trouble and that if he could help I'd appreciate it if he would pass on a message or, better yet, put me in touch.

Yuseff saw this as an opportunity to play out his tough guy image.

"What are you, a fucking cop or what?" he blurted out at a high enough decibel to draw attention to us.

"No, I'm just trying to get some information and I'd like to talk with Donna," I repeated quietly.

"Listen, you jive motherfucker," he said and grabbed me by the collar, "you get the fuck away from me before I kick your preppy ass."

He pushed me and I fell back onto the fence. I didn't think I had such a preppy look, but maybe to him I did.

"I'm sorry," I said and started to walk away.

When I got back to the car I saw him snickering to his friends. As I started up the car Yuseff loud-talked me again.

"I see your punk ass again I'll break your kneecaps, you pussy."

As I drove away, Yuseff was laughing with his buddies.

Despite popular belief, New York City does slow down on Sundays. Midtown may always be packed with tourists but uptown things move at a different pace. Harlem enjoys lazy Sabbath

mornings, although the pace picks up again in the afternoon, after church. My watch read 4:39 P.M., and I realized that I hadn't
eaten all day.

I bought two slices of pizza from a sidewalk vendor on 122nd
and Lenox Avenue and washed it down with a grape Snapple. I
then made a call from my cell phone to a guy named Onion.
Onion is a dangerously gifted computer hacker with a razor sharp
mind who can get into any computer that has ever been made.
He's one of those guys that big corporations wish didn't exist because he knew how to screw up a year of a company's work with
just one click of a mouse button. I felt lucky that he was on my
side. I told Onion what I was looking for from the motor vehicle
department and was told to call back at around 10:00 P.M.

Around the corner on 125th I stumbled onto a movie house
that had caught my attention earlier in the week. The picture
playing that week was part of the movie house's annual African
Film Festival. The film being advertised on the marquee was
called *"Hyenas"* by Senegalese director Djibril Diop Mambety. I
checked the time, then bought a ticket.

The film was good. It was about this old, wrinkled-up rich ex-
prostitute with a golden leg who returns to her impoverished and
dying native village in Africa to punish all the residents who
treated her like dog shit when she was young and poor.

I reached home at 7:16 P.M. and set the radio alarm to bring me
back to life at 9:15. I needed to catch at least a couple hours sleep
because I figured it was going to be a long night. I dreamt about
my parents. Dad and I were in Central Park, the way we often
were when he was alive, listening to a jazz band in the park band-
shell. It must have been an all-star jam because all the jazz greats
were playing together — Louis Armstrong, Billie Holiday, The
Jazz Crusaders, Carmen McRae, Charlie Parker, Miles Davis,
Charlie Mingus; and my mother was on stage too, playing piano.
The same piano that stood in our living room. Mom was playing
with the all-star band. My mother had always played classical music, but now she was playing with Satchmo and the Duke! And

Dad was whistling along with the tune as they played, the way he always liked to do.

The alarm sounded and I woke up with a feeling of deep satisfaction. I had things to do. I reached into the closet and picked up my black utility bag. After beating the dust off, I removed a roll of gray electrical tape, six feet of rope, and a Bowie hunting knife. From an inner pouch I removed a set of brass knuckles. From the kitchen I took a book of matches and a small camera from the cabinet drawer. I checked a can of lighter fluid that I had used at a cookout in the summer. It was the large size and still more than half full. I found a small coffee jar that was almost empty, poured the remaining contents into a clean plastic container, and rinsed out any remaining traces. I then half-filled the coffee jar with lighter fluid, tightened the screw top on the jar, and flicked off the kitchen light.

My watch read 9:57 P.M. as I walked towards a bar named Cepeda's that had a neon Budweiser sign displayed crookedly in the window. The place was small and the patrons were mostly over fifty and Latino. I ordered a Corona beer and told the barmaid in Spanish that I was looking for Marta. She didn't respond and I didn't press her. I knew she had heard me. Marta came over after a few minutes. She was short and fat with a round, pock-marked face. Her red lipstick was smeared unevenly over her thin lips and her short dress looked wrinkled as if she had just turned a couple of tricks standing up in the hallway. I handed her the note Inez had written, along with a twenty-dollar bill.

"You ain't no police, right?" she said. Her voice was surprisingly pleasant. It had a soft, baby doll quality.

"No, a friend, she might be in danger."

"I don't got her phone number and I don't know where she lives either. I used to know but she moved. Last time I saw her, she was hanging in Queens with a guy named CoCo B.

I showed her another twenty.

"I still don't know, sorry "Marta said, then hesitated, "Do you want your money back?"

"Forget it," I told her.

As I turned to leave she said, "Hey, you want me to go out with you to your car?"

"No," I said gently. "Thank you."

I turned and walked away thinking that Marta would probably make more money giving phone sex. A lot of guys liked baby doll voices.

I called Onion, who answered on the second ring. He had the information I needed. After jotting it down in my notebook, I thanked him and hung up.

Dressed in black from head to toe I drove over to 133rd Street and looked for the address Onion had given me. After I had found it, I circled the block three times. When I was satisfied, I parked my car three blocks away and walked back. It was a building with a buzzer security system. I waited near the lobby entrance until someone came out. Before the door closed I stepped inside the building and walked up the flight of stairs like I lived there.

I stopped on the 2nd floor and rode the elevator the rest of the way up to the eleventh floor where I rang the doorbell to apartment 11-G. I waited for two minutes and rang it again, this time longer. Still no answer. I took out a set of lockpicks and within two minutes had opened the door and stepped inside the apartment.

I waited until my eyes adjusted to the darkness then went to work. I found a wooden chair. It wasn't ideal but it would do. I filled two pitchers with water from the tap and then dropped in a handful of ice cubes I took from the freezer. Then I unscrewed the fuses in the fuse box in the kitchen. It was 11:40 P.M. by the time I finished my preparation. I placed the chair against a wall and sat on the floor in the lotus position in the living room.

At 2:00 A.M. I heard a key turn in the lock. The door opened and closed. A single set of footsteps entered the apartment. A hand swished against the light switch.

Nothing.

The footsteps came closer in my direction.

At the appropriate moment, I swung a kick that landed squarely in Yuseff's groin. He dropped to his knees, dazed. Before he could look up I crashed down on the back of his skull with a sap consisting of a five-pound lead weight covered in leather.

When Yuseff came to twenty minutes later, he was butt naked. Then I drenched him in ice water. He shivered from the shock and tried to move but couldn't. His hands and feet were bound tightly behind his back and his body was tightly strapped with duct tape to the straight-backed kitchen chair. Duct tape covered his mouth also.

Then I threw another pitcher of ice water on him. Slowly I moved into the light so that he could see my face. When he recognized the preppy, his eyes grew wide with astonishment, and even wider as I slipped on my brass knuckles. I took my time so he could savor every moment. I hit him flush in the left ribs with all the power I could muster. We both heard the crack of the bones. He moaned, lost his breath, and his eyes rolled back into his head. As he fought to breathe, I repositioned myself and hit him in the mouth. He gagged and twisted as I yanked the tape off his mouth to let him spit out blood and teeth. He tried to scream with pain but, instead, vomited more blood and teeth into his naked lap.

I sat calmly on a nearby chair and started humming Stevie Wonder's "You are the Sunshine of my Life."

Yuseff must have decided that I was one crazy son of a bitch, because when he got his breath back, he started begging in a whimper, "I'm sorry, please, I'm sorry. Don't kill me, sorry, don't kill me."

He must have repeated it twenty times.

I walked behind him and re-taped his mouth, then took the jar of lighter fluid off the table and let him smell it, all the while still humming softly. When I put the lighter fluid under his nose, Yuseff started to cry. I took my camera with special low-light film and snapped three photographs of the jailhouse bully looking wild eyed and helpless with tears streaming down his face. Then I poured the lighter fluid over his head. For about a minute I sat staring at him placidly, still humming, then I pulled out the book of matches. During that minute, Yuseff shit himself.

I spoke in a very calm and polite voice.

"Yuseff, I'm going to ask you a set of questions and I'm only going to ask you one time. I would prefer you give me the answers I want. If you refuse, we're going to have a barbeque. If you choose to answer me with what I find out is a lie, then I suggest that you purchase a life insurance policy with a large death benefit for your mother because I will come back to visit you again, at which time there will be nothing to discuss."

Yuseff said he didn't know where Peter Pan was, but that when he had spoken to her a few days before, she said that she was laying low for a while but she didn't say where.

I told him if, and when, she called to get the number and address, but not to tell her anything else. I also told him that if he should lose track of her whereabouts, I would hold him responsible. I told him to leave the number with Melvin at the Tease Me Club and the message would get to me.

He assured me that he would and, for some reason, I believed him.

I left Yuseff sitting in the dark, tied to the chair in his own waste and crying like a lost calf dying in a thunderstorm.

The fact that Donna Flowers a.k.a. Peter Pan had gone underground told me she was probably an important piece in this puzzle. Just how important I didn't know. I only knew I had to find her.

Randy bit into his third cheeseburger and looked up at me grinning. "I waited up for you brothaman, but you didn't call, so when I didn't hear from you I said to myself, I hope my man is all right, you know what I'm saying 'cause we all right, right?"

Randy could talk a mile a minute and always did. I wondered if he had ever met Sheila. They deserved each other.

"I got busy last night," I told him. "The main thing is you're here now. I want you to find out what you can about these guys."

I pushed the photographs of the two dead Asians across the table in the booth and looked over my shoulder in the direction of the bar. Duke was still filling the stock in preparation for the lunchtime rush.

Randy Miller was a small-time hustler who made money setting up promotion scams, steering prostitutes to johns, and fencing gold chains that had been snatched in the subway by street thugs. But his main source of income came from the New York Police Department or, on occasion, the CIA. Randy Miller was a professional snitch. His defense against doing jail time was that he would rat out anybody for anybody else, so long as they paid him. Another part of his payoff was that the police let him operate his nickel and dime hustles unmolested. He was more reliable than most snitches because he wasn't a junkie, even though he sold small quantities of coke.

The reason I needed Randy was because he knew all the players. He had a knack for making people like and trust him. That was his real talent, and he had contacts from all walks of life. He could have been successful as a public relations man or even a politician. The problem with Randy was, he could never stop thinking like a small-time crook long enough to get something good going for himself. He was the type who would always prefer to steal a crooked quarter than earn an honest dollar.

"Gimme a week," he said still chewing.

"You got two days."

"Two days, that ain't no time . . ." He said still chewing.

"I'm in a rush."

"For the same money, come on. A rush for you means more problems for me. And that deserves a better price, cause . . .

"Same money," I said flatly cutting him off.

"Okay I'll call you in two days," he said. "Same money, two days."

Randy hurriedly finished his burger and left with the photographs.

At least I had gotten a line on Peter Pan. But something else was starting to bug me. Something I needed to do that I had been hoping to avoid. But I knew that I couldn't put it off any longer. I went back into my office and dialed a number in Arlington, Virginia. As I dialed the phone I knew that I was stepping back into my violent past. A past that I had hoped was dead and buried forever.

The voice of a white man with a soft, southern drawl came on the line.

"I'm looking to whip somebody's ass in a golf game so I thought I'd call you," I grinned into the phone.

"Well, come right on 'cause I'm feeling the same way," came the southerner's lazy-like reply. "Well, I'll be damned. How are you?"

Jim Frazier had been my partner in the field and one of my best friends. He still worked for the CIA.

"I'm good. So what about me coming down there to play you some golf."

"Anytime, just come on."

"Wednesday next week at four?"

"Sounds good, meet you at the club."

"See you then," I said and hung up.

Jim and I had been out in the field together as operatives for almost five years, a long time in the espionage business. He had saved my life a couple times, and I'd saved his a couple more. We were real friends.

Since we both knew that calls in and out of the Agency were monitored, we had worked out a code for special circumstances.

This was one of those times.

The message was clear, we would meet at his house that night at 8 P.M.

The drive from New York to Jim's house in Arlington, Virginia, just outside Washington D.C., is approximately four and a half hours. I drove it in just under four. Jim welcomed me.

He was about an inch shorter than me and three years older. Thin and clean shaven with baby blue eyes that conveyed a gentle, unassuming personality, Jim possessed a slightly awkward gait, the result of a spinal injury received in an auto accident that had killed his mother.

Over dinner and drinks I filled him in on the Tease Me Club murders.

"Becoming a real detective, huh?"

"No, just helping my uncle out," I assured him.

"Don't be too sure. It might not be such a bad way to go, at least it would keep you in the thick of things," he smiled across the table.

"A detective? Me? Naw, this is just a one time thing, after this is over I'll go back to running the bar."

"Barnett," Jim smiled. "I know you better than you think I might." He always pronounced Barnett with an open "ah" sound, which made it sound like he was saying "Baahnett."

I changed the subject to inquire about the welfare of his children. He had two: eleven year old William, and eight year old Kurt. Jim had been divorced from Patricia for about three years.

"Everybody's fine. I do the Dad thing on the weekends, which gives Patricia her chance to really do her fire and brimstone thing," he said cheerfully. He had been hurt by the break-up, but there was no bitterness. That's the kind of sweet guy he was.

Patricia was a social worker, who woke up one day and discovered she'd been called by the Lord. After some theology classes from a local bible college, she became ordained and divorced all in the same year. Now she had her own congregation. Patricia was a terribly intolerant and bossy woman who felt black people were quote "special people" unquote whom God had chosen to suffer a little more than the rest of mankind. To back up her point she cited a bible story involving a curse and a character called Ham exposing his brother's naked ass to the world.

I had always felt that Patricia was to religion what cyanide was to a toothache. And I had told Jim as much.

After dinner, I explained to Jim that I needed him to find out everything he could about the Japanese diplomat Katsu Yamaguchi. We spent the rest of the night shooting the breeze and listening to selections from his enviable Charlie Parker collection.

The drive back to New York was restful, it gave me time to think about where I had come from and where I was going. In the past year my life had turned upside down. The fact that Dad was killed was the straw that had broken the camel's back. But the bundle that had brought the camel to its knees was what mattered more. It wasn't any one thing, but rather a combination of a lot of events and circumstances that had built up over a long period of time and came crashing together. My changing feeling about the job, my health problems, my political awakening. The Marcus Barnett who had nobly gone to work in the service of his country fifteen years ago no longer existed. He had died a slow death amid the many years of hellish double-dealings, dirty tricks, and state sponsored brutality. In his place was a cynical Marcus who saw the world as vested interests in expedient situations — peopled with men and women who would blow a man's brains out at noon and sit down three hours later and enjoy a perfectly normal lunch with their families. Men and women who were sanctioned by the government to preserve the American way of life, liberty, happiness, and above all the pursuit of profit at any cost.

I had trained in Silver Springs, Maryland, excelling in weapons and quickly becoming fluent in Spanish, German, French, and Arabic. Why some men feel an overwhelming sense of dedication to their country and others don't I can't say. At the time I joined the Agency, I felt I was doing my bit to keep the world safe for democracy, and free from tyranny, despite the fact that I knew and accepted that racial tyranny existed big-time within the U.S. and the Agency itself. Looking back, I think maybe I felt that what I was doing was so important that race wasn't as important as the job at hand.

My first few years as an undercover agent were spent in Europe gathering information. During my fourth year I was promoted into what was known as the Wet Works Squad. We carried out assassinations, burglaries, torture, and other tactics typically associated with the Gestapo or power hungry dictators. The work was never personal because they taught me . . . to dehumanize the enemy . . . to feel no remorse for those I liquidated . . . to be a soldier in the service of my country. They taught me that it was always us against them. And that God was always on our side.

Within the space of a month there was the assisted "suicide" of an Angolan diplomat in Paris, the assassination of a Senegalese gun dealer, and the brutal interrogation of a Moroccan politician thought to be selling nuclear secrets to China. Increasingly, I found myself destroying the lives of other brown- and black-skinned men, some of whom reminded me of people I grew up with in Harlem. In some ways it was like playing God. Especially after the target had been reduced to a quivering mass of fear and humiliation resulting from a night of torture in some cold, dark room.

It was during this time that I was also being stalled for promotion and pigeonholed by an organization I had pledged loyalty to, risked my life for, and given years of my dedicated service. Admittedly, being passed over made me angry enough to start to resent and question the true motives of some of the cold-hearted bastards sitting behind those CIA desks. Men who never dirtied their hands or minds with the lives of the people they destroyed.

As a black American agent I was always aware of a voice buried deeply in the back of my head when I saw racial injustices taking place. Some days the voice asked "Is it worth it? Are you really making any difference?" And other days it accused. "You're just as guilty as your victims, since you're acting as the oppressor's instrument to aid in the oppression of your own people." As an undercover agent, I could be asked to infiltrate a black organization, sabotage a political movement, plant lies in the media, or even assassinate a black political leader. All in the name of the same squeaky clean democracy that I had never experienced under the U.S. constitution because my skin was black. In fact, I had met pimps with more compassion in their hearts than some priests I knew. I had met thieves with more integrity than politicians I worked and laid my life on the line for.

The most favored path for an agent in the CIA is a few years in the trenches, followed by a junior executive position in a policy-making department. Then you retire with a pension and, hopefully, enough good health to raise your grandchildren before old age takes over.

After fifteen years with the Agency and over ten years in the field, I figured I had done my bit thoroughly and completely in the field and was ready to move up the ladder.

The official response from the CIA administration was that I was too valuable as a field operative and that as soon as a suitable replacement could be developed then I would be promoted. Bullshit. The truth was, the Agency wasn't ready to have someone like me at an administrative level. I was a renegade. My very survival depended on my not being a team player. I had to improvise as I went along. I was a mad dog, a killer on a leash who could not be trusted too close to the things they held near and dear. I *was* the kind of person who could blow a man's head off at lunchtime and calmly enjoy myself at dinner. To have that quality in the trenches is one thing, but to have it in the boardroom is quite another.

Then there was the fact that I was black. One guy in administration actually told me that the powers that be were delaying my advancement for my own good as well as the good of my people. He must have thought my head screwed on and off. I told him that white people didn't even have the right answers to govern their own lives properly, so how in heaven's name could they know what was good for black folk.

So like it or not, I had to face the ugly fact that I was no different than the thousands of other black Americans who had been recruited from colleges starting in the late sixties and early seventies into America's corporate middle management. We were all part of the Great American Integration Experiment, which allowed blacks entry into the system with the unwritten and unspoken understanding that they could rise so high and no higher.

The glass ceiling.

Some days I got so angry and depressed that I thought I just might flip the fuck out like Luke Terrell had done. Luke had been a black agent who showed up at a local police station one night butt naked, covered in blood, and carrying two plastic 7-Eleven shopping bags. Inside the bags were the heads of three of his colleagues with whom he had been on a stakeout. Luke had shot each at point blank range and then decapitated them with a hacksaw.

Where were all those beautiful spacious skies and amber waves of grain that they promised me in the national anthem?

On one of my routine debriefing trips to the division offices I arranged an appointment with a guy in the policymaking department. Marc Dillon. Dillon was just the kind of man that thrived in the Agency. Southern born, educated as a lawyer with degrees from the University of North Carolina and Harvard. A man who could be depended on to misunderstand the most sensitive situations in favor of his own expedient position. In short, a man with a silver tongue and a narrow mind.

The meeting with Dillon had started off pleasantly enough. Yes, he admitted a glass ceiling did exist. Then he assured me that he would pull some strings to remove that glass ceiling if I did him a favor. He wanted me to plant some dirt on a Paul Fleming, who was a well respected powerful black congressman who had gained his power by virtue of being affiliated with the national church community. Dillon explained that the government had a problem with him because he had refused to denounce certain communist enemies of the U.S.

In short, Dillon wanted me to set Fleming up for blackmail. This was an old game, the same game that was used to railroad

Harlem congressman Adam Clayton Powell from power back in the mid-sixties. Congressman Powell had been the most powerful black politician ever. The government set up a policy bag lady to lie. She said that she had given Congressman Powell payoffs. The result was that members of the House voted to strip Powell of his twenty years of seniority in the House of Representatives and his powerful position as chairman of Health Education And Welfare Committee, where he had gained control of millions of dollars going into school districts that discriminated against black people. Of course Adam Clayton Powell's real crime was that he had stood up for black folk and didn't compromise. So when his political enemies found he couldn't be bought or intimidated they railroaded him right out of power. It's as simple as that. Now the Agency was trying to use me to do the same thing to Paul Fleming.

I guess little by little the pressure cooker of ambiguities and hypocrisies had built up in my brain and gestated inside my heart until, eventually, without realizing it, I had given birth to a conscience. Which was something no good agent can afford to have.

When I refused flat out, that bastard Dillon tried to get cute and hinted that the IRS would harass my father. Without thinking I wiped up the floor with him. I broke his jaw and cracked his elbow. My guess is that the University of North Carolina and Harvard had obviously not prepared Dillon for a good old-fashioned Harlem ass whipping.

Security was called and the blood was wiped up. Dad was killed ten days later.

So here I was back in Harlem, with a partial pension and the Be-Bop tavern to run, and now trying to figure out where the hell I could find a young hooker whose street name was Peter Pan.

I was filling a glass with brew at the Be Bop when I looked up and saw a big black cop I recognized.

"Hi, I'm Al Mack," he said, coming over to where I was standing behind the bar.

He didn't really look like much of a detective with his fat bouncy belly, graying hair, and ready smile. For years, Al Mack had worked the beat in Harlem as a uniformed cop and by all accounts he was a straight-up guy. Nobody had ever talked about him shaking down drug dealers or being involved in any burglary rings like a lot of Harlem cops. Now he was in plain clothes. I'd seen him over the years but never had any reason to say much except Hi and Bye. I remembered he was at Dad's funeral. Dad had liked him. On my visits home, sometimes, I'd see him and Dad playing checkers or talking baseball. He was about ten years older than me.

"Wassup," I returned the salutation looking up at him. He was big and roly-poly, but moved on the balls of his feet in a quick, smooth, and easy way that gave the impression that he was some kind of comical Fat Daddy ballet dancer.

"I won't keep you in suspense," he grinned over at me.

"Okay."

"Your uncle called me last night, said you might be able to use my help in your investigation."

I didn't respond.

"It's okay, check me out, I'm legit" he said.

My uncle was right, I could use all the help I could get.

"Okay, give me a minute." I told him. "You want some coffee? Be back in a minute."

I went to the back and called my uncle who confirmed everything the burly policeman had told me.

"Mack is a good man. He's also a friend, I asked him to help you out as a favor to me," Uncle Beans said in a strained voice.

"You sound strange, you okay," I asked him.

"I'm fine, just this damn stomach trouble again. I'll take some bicarbonate of soda later."

"You might need to see a doctor," I coaxed.

"Just indigestion," he said dismissing my concern. "By the way, tomorrow evening if you get a chance, drop by The Hole around eight. We're having a little celebration. Some people I want you to meet." The Hole was a combination private club and gambling joint owned by my uncle.

I told him I would and hung up.

Al Mack was sitting in one of the booths sipping his coffee and reading the sports page of the *Daily News*.

He looked up as I approached and smiled.

"Your Uncle say I was on the level?" he grinned.

"That's what he said."

He didn't look offended, which was a good sign.

I sat down.

"Everybody calls me Mack." He offered his hand and we shook. "So how do you like being back in Harlem?"

"Okay, mostly I've just been learning how to really run this place."

"Any progress on this case?"

"You know how it is in Harlem. Sometimes you never know if you're making progress or not 'cause it's hard to know all the connections."

"That's right, just when you think you got the answer, suddenly something blows up and you find you got to start from scratch all over again," Mack agreed. Then added. "But I think I know where a few bones are buried that might at least put us onto something. I read the police reports."

I went over the details of what I had done so far and he listened intently. He took off his hat and placed it on the seat beside him and rubbed his thick ebony fingers as if the rubbing motion helped him in absorbing the facts.

"Man, we've blown a coupla big cases around here recently because we didn't have the right people handling things," Mack said. "I'm glad they brought you in on this thing."

I knew he was sincere. I told him about Yuseff and Donna Flowers and my theory that she was probably holed up in Connecticut or New Jersey.

He thought for a minute and began to speak slowly and thoughtfully.

"If all a guy had ever eaten in his life was beans, and somebody suddenly walked up and gave him a million bucks, tell me, would he go out and buy steaks and caviar? No, he would just go out and buy bigger and better beans, because beans is all that he knows. That's the way these young people around here think. They could become as rich as cream and still be ghetto. You know, Ghetto Fabulous. To most of these young hustlers in Harlem, Connecticut is way far away, and California is on the other side of the galaxy. This girl we're looking for ain't out of town. She's still right here in Harlem."

His friendly demeanor made him easy to underestimate. But I could tell by the way he talked and approached problem-solving that he was smart enough to use that soft non-threatening way to his advantage in a way that would make him a valuable ally.

Mack's mind was clear and organized. Something I liked and respected. Over lunch we talked about the changes that time had brought to Harlem. He had grown up in Harlem too.

"A few more years, a few more changes," he summed it up and shrugged. "But it don't mean much, ain't nothin changed really since me or you were kids, the white man's still in the lead," he laughed heartily.

"Tell me about it," I remarked dryly.

We talked about people we had known mutually, some who had gone on to better things, some who hadn't. Then Al Mack launched into a story.

"Remember old Joe Grimes who owns the barbershop on 135th?" Mack asked. "Joe is legendary for always being seen with fine young girls. Joe has to be in his late sixties now."

"Isn't he retired? I haven't seen him around."

"Naw, he just got himself shot."

"Shot? When?"

"About six months ago, I was the officer called to the scene. Old Joe got himself involved and fell in love with this young honey about twenty-three years old, and she was driving that old fool crazy. She used to make Joe take off from work just to go shopping with her. What happened is, he was giving her his money and she was giving it to one of them young studs. Joe went to the house one day unannounced, looked in the window of the apartment he was paying for and caught her with some young dude in the bed. His old ass went sho nuff crazy then. He broke the window out with his fist, went in and threatened to kill the guy, but while he was selling those wolf tickets, the girl shot him. Of all places she shot him in the ass. But they made up, so when I get there he covers himself by saying he was making a citizen's arrest. Said he was chasing a guy trying to make a crack bust when he got shot."

"You're lying," I laughed.

"If I'm lying, I'm flying. Ain't no fool like an old fool," laughed Mack finishing off his coffee.

His ready smile and winning way let me know that Mack and I were going to be buddies. Maybe not the closest of the close but certainly close enough and honest enough to watch each other's backs. Our first stop together was the home of Esther Fernandez. One of the dead women. A Latino answered the door. When Mack announced he was the police, the man began stuttering and acting suspicious. He closed the door and said he would go get someone.

"Looks like he's got something to hide," I commented.

"In Harlem, you know many people who don't?" Mack countered.

He was right. Lots of people in Harlem seemed to have something to hide, or were hiding from somebody or something. Hiding from the welfare people. Hiding from a loan shark or a bookie. Hiding from the police or the bill collectors. Hiding from an old boyfriend, or from hunger. People in Harlem were even used to hiding their money in places where members of their own families couldn't steal it from them.

It was five minutes before anyone came back to the door. This time when the door finally creaked open, it was a child's grimy face that appeared.

"Sí?" he asked.

"I'm from the police, I'd like to speak to someone," stated Mack.

"La policía?" he asked with wonderment.

"Sí," answered Al Mack.

The kid slammed the door closed.

My eyes drank in the filthy walls and peeling plaster of the tenement hallway. From inside we could hear him shouting "Mommy, Mommy, la policia, la policia."

The same child reopened the door and disappeared. We stepped inside.

It was a dingy room scattered with old newspapers, kids toys, and various pieces of dirty clothing. From the back of the apartment, a figure came into view.

If anyone could win a prize for looking like something that the cat had dragged in, this woman who toddled from the kitchen into the living room would have won the contest hands down. Long, stringy hair stood wildly on her head giving the appearance of a cave woman in heat. Her sagging, yellowish skin played host to an overstuffed face, marked and spotted by big hairy moles that resembled sleeping cockroaches. She received us with curious bulging eyes and a smile revealing a set of rotting teeth. She was accompanied by a skinny girl child with sandy hair who walked holding onto her soiled dress as if they were physically stuck together.

"Yes," she said with apprehension written all over her face.

"Hello, my name's Barnett, and this is Al Mack, NYPD. We're here concerning Esther Fernandez . . ."

"I'm her mother, but she's dead."

"We know, and we're sorry, but we need to ask you a couple questions concerning any friends that you knew of hers," said Mack.

"Friends?" The woman said the word as if it were the first time she had ever heard it spoken.

"Yes, we're trying to find out who killed her," I remarked sympathetically.

"Killed her?" she said as if it was news to her.

"Yes. She was murdered."

"I know who killed her," she offered.

"You do?" I could feel the adrenaline rushing into my brain.

"Yes, Satan," she stated emphatically, her eyes as hard and black as lumps of coal.

"Mommy, Mommy," a child's voice called her from the other room.

Rapid as machine gun fire, she yelled back to them in Spanish.

"We think that some human might have helped Satan along," said Mack.

"She was a bad girl, God punished her. He let Satan swallow her up, like Jonah and the whale. I warned her. I warned her."

"But, maybe . . ." I tried to interrupt.

"Satan killed her! She was a whore!"

"Do you care who actually killed your daughter?" I asked.

"I don't interfere in God's work." she screamed.

Mack and I passed a look between us. She was a nutcase pure and simple, and it was unlikely that we would get any useful information, so we went back out on the street.

I was well aware that people in Harlem usually knew more than they were telling. Maybe Esther's crazy mother knew something, maybe she didn't. People didn't like giving information to strangers, especially the police. We both figured that Peter Pan was most probably still working her trade somewhere, and quite likely for a pimp named CoCo B.

"I need to swing by the station for a while to check up on some informants and do some paperwork Mack said.

"Cool."

So that's where we headed.

From the corner of 145th and St. Nicholas the distance to the station was thirty minutes walking at a leisurely pace, ten minutes by bicycle, and only seven and a half minutes if somebody was being chased carrying a stolen case of malt liquor. We agreed to meet up again the next day to compare notes or to see if anything had surfaced in the meantime.

Mack went into the station and left me thinking about pimps and whores.

Tuesday, 12:15 P.M.
■ 145th and Riverside Drive

Harlem is more than just a neighborhood: it's a state of mind and a way of life. It's a city within a city, a world within a world. It's history, politics, religion, music, poverty, language, literature, and style, all combined. This quintessentially black American ghetto technically begins at 110th street at the end of Central Park and runs all the way north up to Washington Heights. As avenues 6th, 7th, and 8th pass through Harlem they are re-christened with the names of great black heroes — Martin Luther King, Adam Clayton Powell, Malcolm X, Frederick Douglass. The same goes for Spanish Harlem on the east side, where avenues are re-named after Latino heroes.

I put in a call to Duke Rodgers, my bartender, who had a deep knowledge of who was who in Harlem's street life. Duke quietly made contact for me and set up a meeting with the man I was now on my way to see.

I crossed Broadway at 145th street heading west. Looking across the Hudson River over to Jersey, the sun was starting to set. The effect put a rosy glow on the murky brown water. At Riverside Drive I turned left and drove south to 144th street, where a tall light-complexioned black man with a worn face and dressed in a cheap green jogging suit, a thick gray tattered cardigan, and smoking a cigarette sat on a bench in the park. He was in his late fifties but his hardened and weathered face made him look older.

I pulled over to the curb and sounded the horn. The man bent forward to get a better look. When he recognized me, he ambled toward the car.

"Hey, Doc," Pee Wee said as he opened the car door and climbed inside.

His smile revealed brown stained teeth and breath that reeked of cheap wine.

In his prime, Pee Wee Jones had been a successful pimp with a stable of the finest whores in Harlem. But that was twenty years ago. As a kid I remember seeing him riding in a white Cadillac dressed in pastel suits and accompanied by women who would have looked at home on the Hollywood screen. But like most hustlers of his generation Pee Wee just didn't know when to get out of the life. He hit a streak of bad luck and his house of cards came tumbling down. He ended up with a long bid in the State Pen. Now, Pee Wee was too old to stroll, and without a pot to piss in or a window to throw it out of. The new cars, the thousands of dollars that had passed through his hands, these were all gone now. All the glamour and fame of having once been at the top of his game was all gone, too. Nobody would write any books or articles about him or even give a tinker's damn when his name showed up in the obituary column. All the glory that had once belonged to Pee Wee Jones had been gobbled up by the next generation of young hustlers on the block. Now merely a passing shadow in a Harlem nightmare, Pee Wee was a living testament to the street hustler's life, and the ghetto mentality in general. He was broke, broken, and without a real friend in the world.

In his day Pee Wee was considered a ruthless hustler with a reputation for delivering the goods. Though he didn't have much in the way of formal education, Duke had told me that Pee Wee had a keen street sense that few could match. His instinct for being able to read between the lines in a situation was still razor sharp. Pee Wee could, as the saying goes, look through muddy water and see dry sand.

I explained to him about the murders and how they were done by a professional.

"I heard about that," Pee Wee said. "Jesus got did in that one, right?"

"The Colombian, yeah. Him as well as a whore called China Blue."

At the mention of her name, a smile crossed his street hardened features.

"China Blue, now that is a blast from the past," he chuckled.

"Hungry?" I asked.

"Yeah, I can go for a little somethin'."

We traveled east back to Broadway. On the corner of 145th sat
a small Dominican restaurant called "La Vega." We went in and
took a seat near the back.

We were served immediately by a cute waitress in her early
thirties who wore the name tag Millie. We gave her our orders. I
asked Millie for *arroz con pollo y rojos colorado* (chicken and rice
with red beans) and Pee Wee ordered *bistec con papas fritas y pla-
tanos maduro* (steak with fried potatoes and ripe fried plantains)
and two *Presidente* beers as we waited for our meal. We continued
talking.

"So you think China Blue was down with Jesus who was down
with the Koreans?"

"Definitely," Pee Wee answered. "Jesus had to be using her
'cause she knows gook talk."

"What about Esther, the Spanish whore who was killed?"

"I can't recall her offhand, but as far as the other hoe goes,
you're right, CoCo B would be your man. If she wasn't working for
CoCo, he would at least know who she was working for, or who
her friends would be if he knows this Peter Pan bitch like you say."

"CoCo B huh?" I said.

"Yeah, his real name is Beresford. We used to run together a little back in the day. He was straight pimping them five and dime
type hoes. All he dealt with mostly was Spanish hoes. But guess
what? That motherfucker is damn near old as me and he ain't figured out that the game done changed," Pee Wee laughed. "Ain't
that some shit, he too stupid to realize it. Crack cocaine done
gave straight-up pimping a nosebleed in the ghetto. 'Specially
when crack hoes be trickin for two or three dollars, just to get
enough to beam up, how you gon charge a John a hundred or two
hundred bucks? Can't, unless the broad is straight-up fucking

businessmen in a fancy apartment near office buildings downtown, so the broads can trick when the guys come out on their
lunch breaks. But old CoCo still sleep, he ain't woke up to it yet.
Saw him about a month ago, fool ass nigga riding around in a
rusty ass Volkswagon talkin' 'bout he pimpin'. Hah-hah."

"Hard to teach an old dog new tricks," I said.

"Yep, you right about that," Pee Wee agreed pulling out a pack
of Marlboros. "You want one?"

I shook my head.

Pee Wee popped a cigarette between his lips as Millie arrived
with our coffees.

"No smoking," she said, pointing to a NO SMOKING sign that
was backed up by a city ordinance number.

"No smoking, in a public restaurant? Since when?"

"For a long time now, it's the law," Millie said placing cups of
steaming liquid before us.

"Well I'll be damned," Pee Wee said consigning himself reluc-
tantly to the idea, as he replaced the cigarette back into the pack.
"This city is going to the dogs when they got crazy ass laws like
that, shit we may as well be somewhere in communist China."

The smoking ban in public restaurants had been in effect for
some years, which meant Pee Wee had not eaten out in a long
while.

"Man," Pee Wee began thoughtfully, "that crack shit has killed
and fucked up more people in Harlem than the Vietnam war ever
did. It's a cryin' shame seeing some old motherfucker way up in his
sixties taking his social security check straight to the crackman."

"Yeah it is," I agreed.

"It's a government conspiracy to kill niggas off for good." He
said.

I didn't answer. There had been reports circulating for the past
twenty years that the American government had actively pushed
drugs in the black community and with what I knew about the
CIA I wouldn't have been at all surprised.

Millie brought out a platter with our food. Without another
word, Pee Wee turned his attention to the task at hand. Drench-

ing his steak in hot sauce, he cut his meat into large succulent chunks, then wolfed it down ravenously while shoveling in a pile of potatoes between chews. Apparently Pee Wee hadn't eaten well in a few days and he was making up for it now. He washed his food down with huge gulps of *Presidente* and smacked his lips. He finally looked up at me and mumbled through a mouthful of food:

"You cool?"

I nodded and Pee Wee got busy once more.

He then moved on to dessert, chocolate cake.

"So you knew China Blue?"

"No, not personally, but she's been around for a while. What made her stand out when she came on the scene was her height, she was real tall for a gook bitch. Stone cold hoe, born to it."

"How's that?"

"Natural talent . . . You know how some people are born with a gift for music or fixing cars or athletics. This bitch had a gift for hoeing. I remember one night we was gambling down at Dutchies and an old pimp named Buddy Glass brought her through. Buddy is the one that turned her out. She was just a young thing then, new to the game, but she was turning heads. There was about eight of us altogether, some hustlers playing poker with some businessmen from upstate. Buddy brought her in and put her in one of the rooms off from the main room that Dutchie had set up just for hoes. And I remember, she took on four guys within about an hour and a half. And she really had these businessmen falling for her. A couple of them cats would have married her that night. And then after she tricked with each of them, she came out and sat down to watch us finish our game. She was as cool as ice, composed, and looking as fresh as a daisy, like she had never even laid eyes on a dick. Like she was as straight-up as the fucking queen of England. I'll tell you, I've seen some hoes in my day, but she was bad. Could have gone right to the top if she had a better pimp. If I had her, I would have been a millionaire in a year. But Buddy's problem was the ponies and the blackjack tables. He stayed so far into the loan sharks that he never was able to improve his business."

"I see," I said.

Millie came back to the table and I paid the check

As we walked outside, Pee Wee immediately lit up a cigarette and pulled up the collar of his tattered sweater against the chill of the late October breeze. We walked to the corner together. The sounds and smells of Harlem, as always, up in your face jabbing away at your psyche like a determined prizefighter. As if to remind you that the streets you walked were littered with the struggle to survive all of Harlem's decayed and broken dreams. Small groups of young Dominican men in their twenties and thirties stood in small clumps on the sidewalk talking and laughing. A fat bodega owner waddled out from inside his store and peered up and down the street with a worried expression. Pee Wee's alert eyes swept the street for his next hustle. He issued up a deep resounding smoker's cough and inhaled deeply from the cigarette he held between his ashy fingers.

"Boy, you see this block, these people have really fucked it up with all this Spanish shit," he frowned. Pee Wee was a relic of the old Harlem where blacks stayed in Black Harlem and the Latinos stayed in Spanish Harlem. But all that had changed now.

A beautiful young Latina woman in her early twenties passed by. She was about five foot eight with shoulder length dark hair, brown eyes with beautifully shaped lips, tight Calvin Klein jeans, and a sweater that hugged a pair of perfectly shaped breasts.

"If I was twenty years younger, I would have her working for me," Pee Wee boasted and shook his head with remorse that time and opportunity had passed him by.

"The ghetto mentality is a hard thing to shake," I thought to myself.

"CoCo B got a place out in Queens, lives with his son," Pee Wee told me.

I handed him a ballpoint pen and he scribbled down a number in barely legible handwriting that was one step above a five year old child's.

I reached into my pocket, pulled out twenty bucks.

Pee Wee took the money and nodded. "Thanks for the grub, good looking out Doc."

"Forget it. Just take care of yourself."

We touched fists and walked away in opposite directions, me to my car, Pee Wee to the nearest bodega. Tonight both Pee Wee and I had appointments to see a friend. Only mine would be a person and his would be in a bottle. Pee Wee was merely a passing shadow in an ugly ghetto nightmare.

Driving past posters of an upcoming appearance at the Apollo Theatre by the Wailers minus Bob Marley, something reminded me that I needed to call in for messages.

"Be-Bop Tavern," Duke answered in his dry laconic style. "S'ap-pening Bossman?" he quipped when he heard my voice.

"Just checking . . ."

"Man from the refrigeration company called again and said, wasn't nothing they could do until you found that original warranty card," he told me.

"Damn, all the years Dad had been dealing with these idiots, you would think they would have kept a record."

Duke could sense the frustration in my voice.

"They said, ordinarily they would have had it, but their computer system caught a virus and they lost all their receipt records. Tell you what, you look around at home and I'll have another look around through some old papers down in the basement."

"Thanks. Anything else?"

"Yeah, two Chinese dudes came by looking for you, at least I think they was Chinese."

"Chinese, what did they want?"

"Didn't say, just said they wanted to see you."

"How did they look?" I asked.

"The one doing the asking was about forty, well dressed, spoke English pretty good. The other one didn't say nothing. He was built like a weight lifter."

"Okay, anything else?"

"Naw, that's it."

"Alright, I'll check with you later. If they should come back, ring my cell."

"Gotcha."

I hung up and thought what about what two Chinese guys I knew. The answer was simple. None. A dollar to a donut, this was a piece of the puzzle.

Feeling tired, I drove south towards 125th street and stopped at a red light a block east of the river near Broadway, just under the subway, which actually runs overhead in this part of the city. A McDonald's occupied one side of the street and a KFC held down the other. The rattling above of the 1/9 train that runs north from Battery Park near South Ferry all the way up to Washington Heights, mixed with the lively sounds coming from each side of the busy street. A bag lady walked by pushing a rickety shopping cart that had once been the property of a supermarket. The cart was full of grubby plastic bags, bottles, and dirty clothes. The woman's face was weather-beaten, drawn, and toothless. Her eyes reflected the mad thoughts racing around in her head.

She stopped, lifted her head, and began shouting. Not to anybody in particular, but to everyone in general.

"I told them that Jesus was born in a manger, and they messed up my social security, they got it all mixed up. Ain't that a trip. The most expensive computer ain't nothing, Messed me up so I can't even buy a fish sandwich. Jesus was a fisherman too, hah hah. Messing me around like I wasn't born here. Social security is my right. Ain't no goddamn alien neither. Do I look German to you? Ain't no Nazi. I was born in Tennessee hah hah. The land of the Tennessee walking horse. Ladies and gentlemen step right up."

The crazy bag lady pushed her cart towards 125th, toward the Westside Highway, still shouting. My watch told me it was still early. Just 2:04 P.M.

A plump young man in his early twenties, wearing a dark blue Yankees caps and dirty jeans, came up to the window hawking wares.

"Yo bro, a little something for the body?" he offered holding out a bottle of cologne.

I glanced at the bottle. In New York, you never know what you're buying because the bootleggers are as talented as the manufacturers who make the real thing. That goes for perfume, as well as designer clothes.

"It's the real thing, Cool Water. Check it out for yourself, quality. I can tell you a man of quality by what you drivin', brotha," he said, checking out my powder blue Jaguar. It was about fifteen years old but I kept it in good shape.

"Not today, chief," I said looking him straight in the eye. He read that I was seriously not interested and he immediately shifted his attention to a yellow Jeep that had pulled up behind me. I needed to think.

The various pieces of the puzzle and small bits of conversation were floating around in my head all unconnected. I needed the mental space to allow a logical picture to emerge. Right now my brain was all clogged with the facts. I needed a way to relax and let the logic of the situation fall into place naturally.

The light turned green.

I drove for almost twenty minutes in silence on the Merritt Parkway, a winding road that links New York and Connecticut. Then I turned on the radio, which was tuned to CD.101.9, a mix of classic jazz and the latest releases. In the late forties, Dad had been a bartender at Minton's in Harlem, which was the avant-garde jazz club of its day. It was one of the main places used by the jazz greats like Monk, Dizzy, Bud Powell, and Charlie Parker when they developed bebop. Back then Dad wanted to be a jazz drummer, but after hearing guys like Max Roach and Philly Joe Jones he decided they were way out of his league and stopped. The musicians who had befriended him over the years often stopped by the bar for jam sessions. I got to know them all.

I reached exit 42 for Bridgeport and turned off.

I stopped and bought a bottle of water in a store near the exit, rested a while and took in the cleaner air and the view. Instead of concrete there was grass, instead of buildings there was blue sky. Out here in nature, the thoughts floating around in my head started to gel and I felt better. I took a walk in a park and then started back towards the city.

It was still early, not yet 4:00 in the afternoon, and the autumn sun was brightly glistening through the yellow, orange, green, and brown leaves of the trees that lined both sides of the highway. The beauty of the effect was magical — breathtaking — as Sarah Vaughn massaged my ears with "Moonlight in Vermont." What a voice. Most people don't realize that not only was Sarah Vaughn a fantastic singer, she was also an excellent piano player. Sassy Sarah, as Dad used to call her, had a voice like butter melting on a hot grill.

As I neared the city, I started sorting out the pieces of the jigsaw in my head. First the knowns. To save his ass, Deke would sell his own mother for a dollar and a pork chop. I made a mental note, I decided that when the time was right, I would put my foot so far up Deke's ass, that he would taste shoe polish for a year.

Deke didn't know it but I was probably one of the last people on earth that he wanted to have as an enemy.

The other knowns. All of the other victims, China Blue, the two Koreans, Jesus, the Colombian, the other hooker, were all in the street life. All except Yamaguchi. Why was he the odd man out in this den of iniquity? Normally, if a high-class diplomat wanted to have a hooker, he didn't go all the way up to Harlem. He must have had a real good reason for being uptown.

The next song on the radio was a funky groove put down by Weather Report from the album *Heavy Weather*. I turned up the volume and let the groove take me over for the rest of my trip south along the parkway. Music was my passion as well as my shelter from the storm. I loved to groove to tunes and just lose myself in them. I purposely blanked out every other thought until I saw the sign for the 155th street turnoff. Then I slowly let my mind slip back into the deciphering mode.

The radio launched into somebody's new version of the Lionel Hampton signature tune "Flying Home." The sound of the music blasted me with the thought of something.

I almost forgot Hamp's birthday! My watch read 5:15 P.M.

At 125th, I turned off and almost floored the pedal of the Jaguar. I had to make it across town to see a guy named Omar who owned a toy shop before he closed up for the day, otherwise I was going to be in a jam, big time.

After I had taken care of business with Omar, I stopped by the bar to check the days' receipts. Business was okay. With all the other things going haywire, to know that business was good was indeed a blessing.

I tried not to think about it, but I had started feeling background pain. That's the kind of pain sicklers often have on an ongoing basis. In my case it usually only happened if I was very tired, dehydrated, or under lots of mental stress, which meant there was the chance of a crisis attack coming on. I needed rest. Rest was the best cure. It was six thirty. I decided to catch an hour's nap knowing that it would make me feel better. I unplugged the phone in the office, told Duke to hold all my calls, and conked out.

I woke up in my office at 8:42 and immediately thought about my very important 9:00 P.M. appointment. I was running late. I freshened up and within ten minutes was in my car and heading south towards 110th. My destination was a rundown tenement building at the edge of Central Park. I reached my destination at 9:15 P.M. I parked, took the package that I had bought from Omar's toy shop from my trunk, and walked toward the building thinking that somewhere in Queens was an old pimp named CoCo B who might have a lead on a young prostitute. A prostitute named Peter Pan who saw something important and could explain why an aging prostitute like China Blue and a Japanese diplomat were together at an orgy in Harlem with two Korean hitmen. I called Mack on my cell phone and announced the change to tonight's itinerary based on my conversation with Pee Wee. As I approached the front door other questions popped up, questions like where the hell was the original warranty that Dad had filed away for the broken refrigerator. Questions, yeah I had questions up the ying yang, lots of questions, and no answers.

I rang the buzzer for apartment 4-F. While I waited, I peered through the iron security gate that had been fitted to cover the outside of the plate glass door. The lobby was old and bathed in stark white light that emanated from naked bulbs located at the bottom of the dark staircase and from the corners in the ceiling. The buzzer sounded and I entered. From outside, the lobby looked a dingy gray. Inside, however, the wall and floor were white marble that had gone to seed with dirt and neglect over the years. I opened the door to the elevator and the scent of urine rushed out to greet me as I stepped inside. *Phew!* The gears of the old elevator creaked, moaned, and grumbled like a constipated drunk as it began creeping upwards. At the fourth floor, the door was opened and a tiny pair of arms wrapped themselves around my waist and squeezed tightly.

"I thought you had forgotten, where have you been?" a nine-year-old voice demanded.

I returned the hug. "Never. How could I forget? You should know by now I wouldn't."

The eyes in the face looked at the large package I was carrying and smiled up at me. "Nintendo, right?" Hamp said.

"Right." As I handed him the package from Omar's, I was smiling from ear to ear

Hamp took me by the hand and led the way into the apartment where his birthday party was commencing with at least twenty of his friends and some of their parents.

"Hey baby," Hamp's mother Maxine called to me from across the living room.

"Hey sweet thing," I returned the greeting.

Maxine was surrounded by children with paper plates, all anxious to get their share of the ice cream and cake she was serving up.

Maxine and I had been lovers. Well, let's put it another way: I had been one of Maxine's lovers. Ordinarily that would not have been so unusual. The twist here, is that when she fell pregnant with Hamp she wasn't sure who the father really was. It was between me and two other guys she had been sleeping with regularly. Rather than get a traditional blood test, she decided somewhere along the way to spread the fatherhood of her son between the three of us. The result was that fatherly duties were split between myself, William, and Juba. Interestingly enough, we all stepped up and agreed to become what Maxine coined as "Uncle Daddies."

At first we all thought Maxine was a bit crazy, but time proved that she was a lot smarter than any of us had realized because the results, for Hamp, seemed to be very positive. The boy got the best the three of us could collectively give him. Hamp spent every holiday, school break, and any other free time with one of us. Even when I was in Europe I would send for Hamp. We visited France, Spain, and Italy together. For nine years it had worked out. William and Juba were both cool guys. William was a computer analyst and Juba was a professor of languages. Maxine had always had a thing for what she called "brainy types."

Hamp was fluent in Spanish and a whiz on the computer by the time he was four. Now he was writing computer programs, playing chess, and corresponding in Spanish with pen pals all over South America through the Internet.

The funny thing was that Maxine and my dad had gotten along like a house on fire. Maxine always joked that had she met my Dad first she would be a married woman by now. Dad loved the idea of having a grandchild and Hamp loved Dad as well.

When I arrived at the birthday party both William and Juba were already on the scene and on the job. William was pouring out the milk and juice. "Hey, Dev," he called out. "Jump right in, I could use the help."

"No, I've got something else for him to do," Maxine interrupted.

"Would you mind helping Juba in the kitchen," Maxine directed me.

Juba was as busy as a beaver making sandwiches for the grownups.

"How is it going?" he greeted in his deep baritone voice.

"Okay, okay."

He handed me an apron and I joined in the fun.

Hamp actually looked physically more like Juba than myself or William, but he acted more like William in many ways, quiet and intense.

Maxine always said he had my spirit though.

"Nothing seems to rattle that boy, he just decides what he wants to do, come hell or high water. Once he gets something into his mind — that's all she wrote," she had told me.

In certain ways, I had hoped he was mine, but deep in my heart, in another way, I had hoped he wasn't. At least he would not then have to worry about inheriting my sickle cell disease. That was my biggest fear. I loved him too much to be that selfish.

Juba and I prepared a tray full of sandwiches and passed them around, then we poured out Sangria and Chardonnay for the adults to help wash them down.

With all the going and coming, about forty kids had showed in all. One of the ladies there had twin daughters, her name was Sonia. She was about five foot five and shapely with dark hair and deep-set eyes. She had smiled a few times in my direction and I had smiled back. Eventually we ended up talking and exchanging numbers.

As much as I tried to push all thoughts of work from my mind, for the time being I wasn't having much luck. Sonia's beautiful eyes and her Spanish accent kept bringing me back to CoCo B and how he specialized in Spanish hookers. So here I was, part of my mind on Sonia and the other part on finding a hooker who could lead me to a puzzle dipped in blood.

At around 10:15 P.M. I said my goodbyes to everyone at the party and went back to the Be Bop to meet Al Mack. During our time apart he had come up with an address in Hollis, Queens, for CoCo B.

"Going to Queens ain't my preference this time of night, but I don't see any other way, do you?" Al Mack said.

" Unfortunately, no." I answered.

I decided to ride with Al and two minutes later we were headed toward Queens via the Triboro Bridge.

After traveling for almost forty minutes, we found the house we were looking for. It was a neat, two-story structure on a dead end street. As we approached, we heard an explosion inside.

Mack tilted his large frame up onto the balls of his feet and leaped up the front steps three at a time. I was close behind.

"Goddamit," yelled a man's voice from inside the house

Then came the sound of another gunshot.

Instinctively Mack removed the .38 caliber snub nose pistol from his belt holster and leaned forward. "Police!" he hollered as he sized up the lock to see how best to shoot it off.

The door flew open and inward just as he was taking aim, and a yellow faced woman wearing a long blond wig stood panting and sweating. She looked at us and excitedly pointed inside the house.

"They're trying to kill each other."

Mack and I ran past her.

"Police!" Mack called again, advancing cautiously towards the sound of the commotion.

"I'll go in first, okay?" Mack whispered.

"Don't worry, I got your back," I told him. And meant it.

I saw a baseball bat lying in the hallway and grabbed it.

Suddenly, from out of a doorway flew two men. One was about fifty-five with a stocky build and gray hair. The other man, in his early thirties, was thin and dreadlocked. They were going at each other like crazy, locked in battle like two ancient gladiators. The younger man fell backwards and the older man sensing that his opponent was tiring charged forward using his weight advantage to knock Dreadlocks even further off balance. The younger man held on causing both to crash backwards onto the floor.

"Break it up," Mack yelled out.

The two men kept struggling, paying no attention.

I raised the bat and brought it crashing down on a cheap glass vase in a corner. The sound of glass breaking got everybody's attention.

"Now what the hell is going on here?" Mack demanded.

"He attacked me." The younger man spoke.

"Him thiefing from me," the older man countered, gasping in a thick West Indian accent. "I'll not have it in my own house even if it is my blood. I kill he first."

I immediately saw the resemblance between the two warriors. Father and son.

"You ah liar," blurted the dreadlocked son.

Before the son had time to blink, the father stepped forward and punched him so hard that he went reeling backwards. Mack stepped in between them.

"That's enough now," his voice threatened.

The son regained his balance and stood poised and ready to strike for more action when I stepped forward wielding the baseball bat.

The son paused.

The gray head turned towards the yellow-faced woman standing in the doorway. He was out of breath but still fuming.

"It's your fault, you bitch," the older man said vehemently pointing at her.

"What," she said drawing her almond shaped eyes into slits.

"You heard me," the old man said.

"All of you. Hypocrites, goddamn hypocrites," she spat.

The son pushed his way past his father, past us, and up the stairs. The woman followed.

"Listen, whatever the differences are here, you've got to handle them better than this, otherwise somebody is gonna get seriously hurt," Mack told the older man.

With his barreled chest still heaving, the older man backed up. His eyes were two sparks of passionate anger when he spoke.

"What's your name?" demanded Mack.

"Beresford, Ian Beresford," he wheezed.

"What the hell's going on here?" Mack wanted to know.

"He started it. I come home and caught him in my room going through my pocket book looking for money. My own son stealing from me.

"How do you know he was stealing?" I said.

Beresford's face took on a crimson hue and his voice raised an octave, "I saw," he said pulling down on the skin at the bottom of his eye with his index finger to accentuate the point. "It ain't the first time, you know. Him tief from me to buy dope. He an' she. If you catch a tief in your house, wouldn't you do the same?"

Before I could answer.

Craaasssh!

The sound riveted all attention.

"Raas claat!" Beresford leaped up the flight of stairs three at a time. Mack and I exchanged glances. It was the kind of look that said let them fight it out.

"They can't tell us a damn thing if they're both dead," I reminded him.

When we reached the top of the staircase, the son was standing in his father's bedroom. The father stood motionless, mouth agape with the blood draining from his face and eyes staring in disbelief through the gaping hole in the room's large picture window. Down on the street below were the remnants of a brand new big screen TV. It lay broken in a thousand pieces.

"Buuumbaclaat," Beresford shouted like he was some ancient warrior leading his troops into battle. The woman with the yellow face stood there looking blankly and would have continued to do so had Beresford not slapped her so hard that she flew into the wall. The father had wanted to hit the son again too, but Mack was between them, which put him out of range; so the woman was the next best thing. I grabbed the old man around the neck, hoping to divert his rage. But I never suspected that the old boy was as strong as a Georgia plow mule. In one deft motion he flung me over his shoulder into the wall. A lightning bolt of pain shot through my back and I was disoriented for a moment. Mack held the woman who had now joined in the kicking and screaming and was trying to get at the father.

I am not sure how it happened, or when it happened, but the next thing I knew the old man had lifted the son above his head and had thrown him hard against a wall. I accepted then and there that I was about to see a killing. The son's face contorted in pain. He tried to scream but there was no sound. When it finally did come, "Ooooooh God!" his voice wailed like a cat o' nine tails was whipping his naked skin. Mack was closest to them and I was still on the floor. The father's right hand was locked onto the crotch of his son's pants. A trail of blood seeped through the son's white pants. The son passed out but the father kept holding on tight. Mack lifted the revolver high above his head and with all the strength his two hundred and sixty three pounds could deliver brought the butt of the pistol down against the back of the old man's head.

At first, Beresford didn't seem to feel anything. Mack raised his hand ready for another blow, and the old man turned around slowly with his eyes glazing over and looked straight up at Mack. His gray head fell onto his chest and his body went limply down onto the hardwood floor, out cold with his eyes still open. Mack looked over at me. I shrugged my shoulders. We had just come by to ask a few questions and had walked into World War III. That's New York for you.

Mack and I waited for the paramedics to load father and son into the ambulance. Both were still out cold. The ironic part of it was that they would ride in the same ambulance and probably wind up in the same hospital ward, side by side. The chill of the evening shot through my body and made my aching shoulder hurt even more. Somebody had called the police and as the paramedics drove up, so did two squad cars. Kelly, a red haired, freckle faced sergeant came over and got the details of what had happened from Mack. Kelly was chain smoking Marlboros like a chimney. He said he had been trying to quit and claimed to be winning the battle, but the way I had it scored, the nicotine had him in trouble against the ropes.

"How you feel?" Mack wanted to know. I guess I had started to look a little green around the gills. I was tired and aching.

"Just a little sore, but I'll be all right."

"For good measure, get the doc to look you over."

"I'm all right," I repeated. At least I hoped I was.

"This domestic violence stuff is always a headache," said Kelly.

"Yep," stated Mack dryly.

By now Joe Public had gathered around for a better look-see.

"Who got killed?" one man asked.

"Just be glad it wasn't you," someone else answered.

Other oblique faces loomed from windows and around corners. Residents have a way of not wanting to be too visible when the police are on the scene.

Within ten minutes the ambulance pulled off with us following behind in Mack's black sedan, sirens blaring and heading for the hospital. Shootings, muggings, stabbings, hot-lye baths, ground-glass meatloafs, and drug overdoses were among the more common reasons why ambulances race through the streets of New York.

The E.R. staff who met the ambulance were professional, quick, and thorough. Father and son were expressed through the halls away from public view and behind green curtains. As Mack and I tried to follow, a nurse with a set of breasts that looked like two giant torpedoes, and a small scar above her top lip, stopped us.

"You can't go back there," she said looking us over suspiciously.

"Police," Mack said flashing his badge. "This is official business."

"You can be Nelson Mandela for all I care," she said nastily.

"You have to get a pass from the front desk otherwise I get into big trouble."

Mack started to argue but I guess something in the woman's demeanor made him decide against it. I know I would have. She reminded me of a Russian lady wrestler I once knew who had gotten arrested by the authorities for whipping her husband's ass. She had cracked him in the head with a frying pan and knocked him clean into a five-year coma.

We got passes from the thin-framed woman at reception taking care of her green, four inch fingernails and made our way back past the nurses station towards the emergency room. In the end, the doctor told us they treated the son for a ruptured scrotum and old man Beresford for a concussion and that both were being kept in overnight for observation.

"Some dumb luck. We go just to sniff something out and wind up almost knocking a guy into kingdom come," Mack said. "Worse part is I'll probably be up half the damn night with the paperwork."

Beresford had been moved into a semi-private room on the third floor. He must have had good medical insurance. We rode the elevator up and stepped out into a hallway that smelled of medicine and industrial strength disinfectant. His room was at the end of the hallway.

Two patients occupied the room. Nearest to the door was a large black man sleeping in a fetal position with a clear plastic tube running from his nose to a machine. Past him on the far side, Beresford lay flat on his back with his head bandaged. He looked up as we approached and, recognizing Mack, pulled an ugly frown.

"What the hell you want?"

"Just a few questions," Mack answered.

Beresford's face contorted in anger as he struggled to sit up in bed. His rich baritone voice rose in pitch, almost to soprano.

"You bust me head, try to kill me, and now you harass me. I ain't tellin you no damn thing."

"I hit you to keep you from committing murder, it's my job, I'm a cop."

"Humph."

"As the old saying goes, we got ways to make you talk," I added. For the first time Beresford focused on me.

"You the one that jumped me from behind?" he said glaring at me. "You don't scare me. I'll call the doctor and I'll call my lawyer too. This is police brutality. I will sue."

I walked to the entrance of the room and closed the door. Then I walked back over to Beresford's bed and picked up a pillow.

"I might just cover your face with this pillow until you stop breathing, you no good, half-assed, would-be-pimp," I said, moving the pillow close to his face.

Beresford looked at Mack who just smiled back sweetly. Fear suddenly found a place Beresford's eyes.

"Just a few answers to a few questions and you can go off to beddy bye," Mack said. "What do you know about a hooker named Donna Flowers? Now, before you fix your mouth to lie, we know that she's been tricking for you. We also know that you turned her out, which means if I feel up to doing the paperwork, you could be looking at five to ten in the state pen, easy. With your past record, I'd say more like ten. So take your time, okay Pops? Where can I find her?"

The more I got to know of Mack the more I liked him. He was like a smiling cobra, affable but deadly.

"She told me that someone was lookin to kill her, that's all what she told me." Beresford was ready to talk, but not quite sure of where to start.

"Where is she now?" I asked.

"Don't know. She come t'rew me place las' night, needin' money, but she didn't tell me where she's stayin,' honest, but after she left she call back about an hour later from a phone booth that had a Harlem number exchange."

"You give her the money?"

"No mon. She used to work for me, but no more. She get hardheaded and start dis fuckerie selling drugs. I not inna dat."

"But ain't you supposed to be her pimp? How she just leave with no strings attached."

"Lissen, I notta beat up onna woman, pimp you know. I a businessmon."

"What about the U.N., you working any girls down there?" I asked.

"Yeah, lots of steady customers dere, mon. Quality."

Mack and I passed a look between us.

"You know if she ever dealt with a Japanese diplomat named Yamaguchi?" Mack asked.

"I don't know no Yamaguchi. I gotta memory like an elephant. I got dat kinda brain, I don't write nothin down. Never no Yamaguchi," Beresford said shaking his bandaged head.

We left Beresford and headed back to the Be-Bop Tavern.

"Think he was being straight with us?" I asked, looking at him across the bar.

Mack nodded affirmatively.

"More or less, he's a two-time loser. He ain't got much choice. He goes to jail again, no chance of parole. He'll do every day of his sentence, which in his case could be life."

Mack was silent while he finished his second beer then said,

"You know we might luck up and find some answers if we can get a few breaks."

"Yeah," I agreed. "We just might at that, cheers."

I had to admit, Mack had been right. If beans was all that a man had ever eaten, then beans was all that he knew. Peter Pan was still somewhere in Harlem.

*H*is angel's voice reached deep down inside him, touching things that had never been touched in him before. Her brown back arched high as she rose and fell again and again on top of the man with the dead eyes who gasped for breath and tasted the sweat of her body. Simultaneously they climaxed then fell apart panting. The angel looked down at the man with the dead eyes. It was an ugly, lopsided face. His features were hard and drawn. His hands were rough and brittle and his breath always smelled bad. He wasn't the type she would have normally chosen. But his strong body and mindless devotion was what she needed now. He was all she needed now. She told him to go get into the tub. The man with the dead eyes obediently did what his angel told him. He always did. The angel looked around. There was a hot plate on the windowsill, a refrigerator, a bed, two chairs, and a dresser in the small dingy furnished room. No radio, TV, or table to eat on. The angel's perfume filled the room, creating a kind of magic for the man with the dead eyes.

But terror had found its way inside the bathroom, amid the steam and the hot water. He believed that the water in the tub had turned to blood. He tried to call the angel to come get him, but she could not hear him. The screams inside his head were too loud and the voice in his throat was paralyzed. The monsters of fear and madness were holding him firm and refused to let go. He prayed for the angel to come. Inside his head, his brain cried out.

From the other side of the door, his angel heard him scream. She tried to open the door, but could not. The angel quickly wrapped a sheet from the bed around her naked body and ran to the apartment next door. She needed help. The old man, Mr. Willie, followed her back into the apartment. Once inside the angel let the sheet drop. The sight of the angel's naked body made Mr. Willie almost choke on his cigar.

"*Holy Jesus*," *he managed to mutter just before the upper plate of his false teeth hit the hardwood floor and slid across the room. Together they pushed against the door until it gave way. Through the steam, they could see the man with the dead eyes. He was sitting on the floor moaning and looking out into space as if in a trance. The angel comforted him by rubbing his naked body and whispering into his ear until he came out of the stupor. Mr. Willie just watched.*

"*You got to do it today, today,*" *she kept saying to him as she kissed and held him on the bathroom floor.*

"*Yeah, baby baby,*" *Mr. Willie began rubbing his own penis through a hole in his trousers pocket. Though his mind was racing with erotic excitement, Mr. Willie's penis remained as soft as cotton candy. Mr. Willie, who was eighty-four, thought about a pretty woman he had made love to some twenty odd years ago when he had been in Kentucky for his brother's funeral. He reached way, way back for the memory of them making love. All the while they had made love she had kept calling him Daddy, Daddy, Daddy. Still, nothing. His eighty-four year old penis was stuck on soft. He continued to watch the naked couple, but after a while got mad and went back into his own apartment.*

The angel had forgotten about the little old man from next door. When she came out of the bathroom, he was gone. The angel led the man with the dead eyes back to the bed and they made love again.

"*You're going to have to do it, do it tonight. I've been good to you, so I want you to do what your baby say to do. You have to do it tonight. Do it for your baby. Otherwise the plan won't work,*" *the angel told the man with the dead eyes.*

She reached down into the bag she carried and brought out the brown bottle that held the magic elixir.

"*Okay, okay,*" *was all that he said.*

The angel used the brown bottle on him and took all the remaining pain away. The man with the dead eyes felt love wash over him. He had never experienced this feeling for anyone before. Not even for his mother, the mother who left him a long time ago with ten dollars in Big Sam's house. Only his angel could make him feel this way.

The sun was sliding from its place in the sky when the man with the dead eyes drove to the place in Harlem on 125th street where a Korean man named Mr. Lee owned a sportswear store. From his car he could see inside. Most of the customers were black teenagers dressed in baggy pants, tee shirts, and oversized leather jackets. One guy was outside using the glare of the large storefront window as a makeshift mirror to examine a haircut that consisted of three parts on one side, the initials D. D. on the other side, and a fade in the back. Two men in their early twenties driving a new Mercedes Benz pulled up next to him. Neither one of them paid him any attention. All of their concentration was on the rap music pumping out of speakers with the bass turned up. He saw the Korean man who owned the store, then drove away. Now he had everything he would need to do what his angel baby needed him to do.

He drove downtown to 74th and Broadway near the old Ansonia Hotel and parked on 73rd Street between West End Avenue and Riverside Drive. The street was lined with well-kept apartment buildings. The people walking along the street looked decent and respectable. Even the dogs looked free from worry. Life here seemed manageable, not like in Harlem where everybody and everything looked like they were caught up in the fight for survival. Not like Harlem at all.

Walking west, the man with the dead eyes reached a tall brick building with an entrance leading to an underground garage. Nobody noticed him go in through the side door. He found a dark corner of the garage and settled there amid the smell of old motor oil and the muffled sounds of the city and waited.

When the car he awaited appeared, it was in the dead of night . . . Inside a light blue Ford sedan was the Korean who owned the sportswear store in Harlem. He was not alone. On the passenger side was an Asian girl. She looked young, twenty-one or twenty-two. They were talking. The man with the dead eyes didn't try to hear their words. He concentrated on their movements as they locked the car and began walking towards the elevators. The man with the dead eyes moved smoothly and effortlessly like a cat through the semi-

darkness. *The blinding pain came to the Korean store-owner without warning. He gasped more in surprise than in pain as the man with the dead eyes rammed the Bowie knife deep into his soft flesh, puncturing his right lung. Blood gushed from the Korean and sprayed the front of the assassin's army fatigues as the young woman watched her father die. Terror froze her vocal chords. She tried to run but the man with the dead eyes was faster. He reached out and caught a handful of her thick black hair and spun her around. Her terrified eyes met a black, sweating face disfigured by an uncontrollable, burning rage. His eyes were two flaming cannonballs in white saucers. She clawed at his hands and bit his arm to get away, but he was too strong. Hate had coiled around his heart like a serpent and slid down through his heavily-veined black hands and into his fingers, which gripped her throat and held it like a vice. Suddenly, her neck snapped, and life came to a screeching halt. She was dead. Cemetery dead. The dead girl satisfied a hunger inside the man with the dead eyes. Killing unleashed a sensation inside his brain. Like the summer rain it refreshed his psyche. He looked down at the lifeless girl and jarred some long ago distant memory of a high school sweetheart that he had forgotten to love.*

I was tired. Christine brought my coffee over to the booth and sat down. Normally she wouldn't have been in the bar this early, but I had asked her to come in. I had worked out a schedule that would allow her to cover for me during the extra time I had to be away.

"Since Duke don't want the job, why don't you just make me the assistant manager. I got a few ideas that could improve this place," she said.

"That's what I had been planning anyway, I just hadn't had a chance to tell you." I smiled.

"For real?" she said excitedly, puffing up with pride.

"By the way, those extra hours that you'll need to have to pay for someone to watch your kids. Have the baby-sitter make out a receipt then take it out of petty cash."

"Thanks." Then she added with a laugh, "I had better ask for the moon 'cause you're on a roll this morning. Whatever it is you been taking, make sure you don't run out, I could get used to days like this." She grinned.

I was glad that I could show her my appreciation. Christine and Duke had stood by and helped me to make the Be Bop run after Dad had died. Duke had been around for years and years. Christine had only come on after I had taken over.

I expected a call from Mack by the afternoon, so when the phone rang at 1:00 P.M. I thought it would be his voice on the other end, but instead it was Melvin.

"Somebody named Yuseff called and said to call him. He left a number."

"Thanks. How long ago did he call?"

"Just about five minutes."

"Thanks," I said and hung up.

I called the number and Yuseff's voice came on the line.

"This is the preppy . . . What you got?"

"Uh yo, she called me about an hour ago," he said in a slow voice that sounded as if he'd been drugged.

"And?"

"We suppose to hook up tomorrow. She say she gon' call me in the morning."

"Why'd she call?"

There was a silence on the line. I could almost hear him thinking. Did he want to open himself up to me totally or was he willing to run the risk of getting another visit in the middle of the night.

"Why did she call?" he repeated the question.

"You a tape recorder or what Yuseff. If your memory ain't working, I can help you,"

"S-Sh-She needed cash," he stammered.

"When and where?"

"I ain't sure yet."

"You set the place," I told him. "And tell her you need her to meet you there exactly on time otherwise you can't help her. And you call me tomorrow as soon as she calls you. Here, take this beeper number. When you call use the code 888, and I'll know it's you, got it?"

"888, right," he said. Then he repeated the beeper number. Yuseff was playing it straight. He wanted to live.

"Okay."

"Yo, brotha," he said.

"What?"

"I was only playing around with you. I didn't really mean those things. I just wanted to apologize. I'm fucked up. The doctor put me on drugs and I lost eight teeth. I'm fucked up. I was just playing, I didn't mean none of what I said, you know what I'm saying."

"Yuseff, that will teach you, I don't play," I said and hung up in his ear.

The phone rang again five minutes later. This time it was Al

Mack who asked me to meet him in Varney's office in an hour. I said okay.

Perhaps things were coming together in some way. I didn't know exactly what Peter Pan could give us but I knew she would give us more than we had. Exactly thirty minutes later I walked into the police Captain's office.

"Cigar?" Varney offered, picking up a stogie from the box on his desk.

"No thanks."

"What have we got so far?" he wanted to know.

"It's still early yet," Mack told him.

"I need results fast. The pressure is on from downtown. It's been a week since the murders."

"What makes you think we can accomplish miracles, or do you still believe in the tooth fairy?" I spat.

I sensed that Al wanted to laugh.

Varney chose to act like he didn't hear me. Instead he popped an ulcer pill into his mouth and started chewing, then pressed on pompously.

"I don't know that I can keep a lid on this thing much longer. Deke told me . . ."

I cut him off in mid sentence.

"Fuck Deke. Listen, your whole goddamn police force can't break this case, that's why you asked me in. No, correction, dragged me in. Tell you what. I see where you and Deke are coming from, you guys want to spill the beans. But I found out about a few beans I could spill too. A few things that would take the attention away from the diplomat killing and lay everything right at your doorstep. You don't believe me, let's go head to head and we'll see," I said, displaying exactly the kind of loose cannon attitude that professional ass-kissers like him were deathly afraid of.

Varney's eyes narrowed in a flash of anger. He wasn't used to anyone pulling his chain the way I did.

"We'll find out something as quick as we can, Captain," Mack said, hoping to diffuse the tension.

Varney just looked at me then ate another ulcer pill. This time he chased it with a cup of water sitting on his desk.

"I just thought you'd have something, that's all. Anything is better than nothing. At least something that would keep the hounds at bay." He directed his statement toward Mack, who was clearly the more congenial.

The door to Varney's office opened. A female sergeant poked her head inside.

"Sorry Captain, I know you didn't want to be disturbed," she said, "but it's Assistant Commissioner Fazio on the line. He says it's urgent."

Varney said "Okay put him on." Varney looked at us. "Excuse me for a minute.

Mack and I walked out of the office and waited by the door. The precinct buzzed with its usual menagerie of hustlers, pimps, whores, gamblers, dope men, stick-up artists, partygoers, barflies, con artists, wild teenagers, bums, thieves, professional snitches, and anyone else who traded in every kind of vice imaginable. I looked back through the glass window of the office as Varney's face contorted into a tight grimace as he held the telephone to his ear and spoke. I could hear him faintly through the door.

"Goddamn," he explained. "Maybe so, okay," he said into the receiver then hung up.

A few minutes later Varney motioned us back in with a wave of his arm.

"Looks like today may be your lucky day," he said turning toward me. "This morning they just found two Korean bodies in a garage. The coroner reported that the wounds are identical to the ones on two of the victims from last Wednesday night. From the looks of it, he used the same weapon too. They put 'em on ice already," said Varney. "Mind having a look-see?"

"Why not."

"Man you are something else. I see I can learn a thing or two from you," Mack smiled as we walked towards his sedan. "You got old Varney shitting green whenever you press his button."

"I've had a lot of experience with the Varneys of the world. They only understand one language, you kick their ass or they kick yours."

"Good observation," Mack chuckled and turned his sedan into the south-bound direction on the FDR.

Polonski was out sick, so one of the morgue attendants showed us the bodies.

"A little chilly in here, huh?" Mack said.

The man grinned. "Don't seem to bother the stiffs none though," he smirked enjoying the chance to crack his well-worn joke. He pulled out the drawer and uncovered a pretty, young Asian woman with a broken neck.

The coroner's report indicated a clean break on the upper section of the spinal cord. The same as Esther Fernandez.

"Ready to see the other one?" asked the attendant.

I nodded. The attendant pushed in one drawer and pulled out another.

The dead man, John Lee, had one killing wound, with a hunting knife. Straight through the lung. The same as the big Asian. The mark of a pro. Maybe there were a few things to rethink. Okay, so maybe this thing is bigger than just what happened in Harlem. On the other hand, the Korean was the owner of a store in Harlem. My inner sense told me the answer but I could not crystallize the feeling into an articulate thought. Not yet anyway. I was still working on instinct. Nevertheless, all of the events that had taken place were not random, they were connected in some way. Then the familiar words of my grandmother came back to me. When things fell into place too easily she had a favorite saying, "There ain't that much coincidence in the world."

Mack drove me back to the Be-Bop. He had to go home. His eleven-year old son was playing junior league football. He was first string quarterback and tonight was the first game.

"If I don't make this one, I'm going to have to find another place to live," he said. "I'll check with you first thing tomorrow."

Mack rode off with his mind on junior league football and I checked my messages to find that Randy Miller had called. He left a number for me to call him back.

"Sonny's Place," a female voice answered. I asked for Randy who came on the phone laughing.

"My man, I been hustling my black ass off for you. Man, you have no idea of the shit I've been through, but you know me, right. You know I wouldn't leave you hanging, I wouldn't. That ain't me, right, you know that."

Randy as usual, was talking shit a mile a minute. He gave me a number in the 718 exchange.

"Call my man Billy out in Queens, he'll hook you up."

"He'd better."

"Naw, everything's cool," Randy assured me. "He will."

I called the number Randy had given me and asked for Billy. Billy answered the phone and said that I could come out today. The sounds of Miles Davis playing "My Funny Valentine" serenaded me all the way out to Queens. My destination was the neighborhood of Flushing, Queens, which runs north to south for about three miles from Roosevelt Boulevard down to Horace Harding Parkway. Main Street in Flushing is a flurry of mostly Korean and Chinese stores and businesses. I went to the address Billy had given me and rang the bell. After a few minutes a young Asian woman's face appeared from behind the glass.

"Yes?" she said acting extremely cautious. A black man in this heavily Korean and Chinese part of Flushing was somewhat unusual to say the least.

"I'm looking for Billy Kim."

"Billy Kim, why?"

"I have business with him. Police business."

"What police business?"

This woman was starting to get on my nerves.

"Listen, I'm from the police department. If I don't speak with him everyone in your house could wind up in serious trouble," I told her.

The caution in her eyes turned to indignation. "Hold on," she said and left abruptly.

About two minutes later Billy came to the door. He looked out from behind the glass with a worried look.

"Who are you?" he wanted to know, with irritation in his voice.

"I just spoke with you about an hour ago. Randy Miller's friend." Billy's face broke into a smile.

"Oh, okay." He yelled something in Korean over his shoulder to cool the lady out as he opened the door. "Come in," he said.

Billy Kim was a round faced Asian man in his early thirties with a short haircut and beady eyes. He wore a blue and white Fubu sweatsuit with black Nike running shoes.

"You scared the shit out of my sister, man," Billy chuckled looking me over.

"Why didn't you answer if you knew I was coming?"

He grinned, causing his eyes to almost disappear into his plump face.

"I don't like to always let the left hand know what the right hand is doing," he said. "You know how it is."

Looking at Billy, the old saying that "Birds of a feather flocked together" was ringing truer than ever. Billy was a Korean version of Randy Miller, a professional small-time slimeball bullshitter. Two peas in a pod.

We went upstairs to his bedroom. It seemed more like the room of a teenager than a grown man. It was filled with records, pornographic videotapes, and rap and rock music CDs. The walls were adorned with photographs of sexy looking women from TV shows that had been cut out of magazines. Billy told me the photographs of the dead men I showed him were indeed the photographs of two men who worked as tough guys for various Korean gangster types. The big Asian man and the one-eyed man were brothers formerly known to the world as Robert and Henry Kim, a.k.a. The Catastrophic Kims. They did a lot of collection work for the loan sharks who financed Korean-owned vegetable stands that had been springing up in New York over the past twenty years. He explained that the syndicates were very good for Korean immigrants who wanted to bring their families to America. The gangsters would set the families up in business in return for a big piece of the action.

"Is that all?" I asked.

He shrugged. "All Randy said you wanted was names and what they did. He didn't pay me for nothing else."

I was right, he was the Korean version of Randy. He wanted to up the ante.

"I want to know who they were working for and why they were up in Harlem."

"A hundred bucks," he said.

"Okay."

I reached into my pants pocket and pulled out one of the packets I had prepared for the occasion. I had learned to always come prepared when dealing with informants. They always wanted money, and they could always be made to give more than they planned to if you showed them the cash. By nature, informants were greedy. I had known countless informants who had either turned up dead or who just never turned up. Mostly because they became too greedy. Asian gangsters were known throughout the underworld for their brutality against informants. For them, torture went with murder like bacon went with eggs. Billy no doubt was aware of the reward-to-risk ratio of his profession. I passed him the money.

"Now, I don't know exactly why they were in Harlem, but I can tell you this. They worked regularly for this real estate company that leases the places that the vegetable shops operate in. And they had been expanding in Harlem."

"The name of the company?"

"Sun Bright Reality. They have offices down around Wall Street I think."

"That it?"

"That's it."

"Did Randy tell you about me?" I asked. The reason was pure

and simple. If he lied to me, I would be back to pay him a little visit one night like I had paid Yuseff. Just like old Mary Mack all dressed in black.

"Yeah, he said don't fuck around with you unless I wanted to find myself in a body cast."

"He was being kind. I was thinking more along the lines of the East River," I corrected.

Billy Kim was trying to play it cool by laughing off my comment, but I saw that he swallowed hard and the lump almost caught in his throat. Message received.

When I crossed back into Harlem it was almost 8:30 P.M. I was tired and my mouth was very dry, which was a sign of dehydration — a very bad sign for a sickler. I really needed a couple days rest but I had also needed to make good on my promise to Uncle Beans.

"The Hole" occupied the basement of the Kingston Arms apartment building. The main floor of the Kingston Arms housed the Harlem Children's Foundation. This was a place where poor parents could bring their children to daycare for a nominal fee. It was partially funded by the state and federal governments, and it was well run by Mrs. Geneva Cox. Mrs. Cox was a frail looking, no-nonsense woman with an ego the size of Alaska. But she was good at what she did and that was all that mattered to Uncle Beans, who happened to employ Mrs. Cox as well as own the building. The basement, which had been redesigned more than twenty years ago into a casino, consisted of two large rooms decorated recently in lush gold carpeting, white walls, and real crystal chandeliers. It had a private entrance that led to a hallway and came out into a huge room filled with roulette tables, slot machines, and all of the other things one would expect to find in a proper gambling casino. It also catered to games like "Tonk" and "Bid Whist" that black folk enjoyed playing. Harlem residents had named the casino, "The Hole."

Kit saw me enter and came over to greet me right away.

"So what's the big occasion?" I asked my cousin.

"You'll see in a minute, you are just in time."

She led me into one of the side rooms that had been laid out with a sit-down dinner for the occasion. In the middle of the table was a cake. My uncle sat smiling at the head of the table and to his right sat a woman I'd never seen before. She looked to be in her late forties or early fifties. She had caramel colored brown skin, wore a shoulder length page-boy hair cut, and an expensive black dress that dipped at the neck over a pair of smooth shoulders. A pretty middle-aged woman. I was introduced. Her name was Barbara Simmons.

"Please to meet you," she said in a deep, rich contralto that had a beautiful tonal quality that conjured up images of thick maple syrup. Her eyes twinkled as she greeted me. There were about twenty people in all and I knew about half of them. Little Phil, the casino manager; Tall-Paul, my uncle's old fishing buddy; Miss Pritchard; Mrs.Cox; Ella Nixon; Reverend Potter; Shelby Green; and Amir Hassan. We ate, drank, talked, and laughed for about an hour. Then my uncle stood up, cut the cake, and announced his engagement to Barbara Simmons. Everyone participated in the hip hip hooray cheer and sang "For he's a jolly good fellow." Reverend Potter asked the blessing of the Holy Father for the couple. All in all everyone seemed to have a good time. Even Kit seemed to accept her father's engagement to this woman. I stayed for about and hour and left. My body was talking to me.

On my way home I reflected on my uncle's new-found happiness and thought that maybe now it was also time for me to settle down too. The next thought wasn't a conscious one, but it came up out of nowhere to jab at me. Amanda. There she was again. Always a barrier to some future emotional involvement. I knew one day I'd have to deal with all of that emotional turmoil before I could move forward. One day I hoped I'd be able to find the strength to deal with this emotional roadblock once and for all. One day.

Thursday, 10:36 A.M.
■ Corner of 133rd and Lenox Avenue

I waited on the northeast corner of 133rd Street and spoke into my cell phone.

"You ready?" I asked. "Yeah," Yuseff said.

"Did she agree to the place?"

"Yeah, I told her the Laundromat around the corner from the park, right? She know exactly where the spot is."

I had named the place in case Yuseff decided at the last minute on a cute little ambush. Even if he did, Al Mack was in another car with a walkie-talkie. Backing Mack up were two more detectives from the precinct. Five minutes later Yuseff came downstairs. He drove his 4x4 to the Laundromat. I followed at a safe distance. I was driving Christine's car just in case he remembered mine from our first meeting. He got out and looked around for me. But I was nowhere in sight. I decided to stay concealed until Peter Pan showed. Five minutes later she arrived. The young woman and Yuseff embraced outside on the street in front of the Laundromat and went inside. I waited a few minutes. When I felt everything was on the square I gave the signal to Mack. Mack in turned signaled his backup to move into position and walked into the Laundromat. I waited until he was inside before I followed.

The place was a large oblong-shaped room with dryers on one side and washers on the other. There was a sink in the back and a bench that ran about half the length of the room. Through the dirty window I could see Yuseff talking to Peter Pan. After seeing her, I understood how she got her nickname. She was about five foot even and wore a short haircut that reminded me of the Beatles circa 1962. Peter Pan's features were plain and she could have easily been a feminine boy, or a boyish woman, take your pick. The place itself was empty except for two old ladies. I walked inside and locked the door behind me. One of the ladies looked up and grimaced. What I was doing had all the markings of a robbery. I walked over and whispered that I was the police and to just sit quiet. She did as I asked. At the right moment, I signaled Al Mack and he moved in. He walked up to Yuseff and announced himself.

"Move out Yuseff. Donna, my name is Officer Mack I'd like to talk to you."

Yuseff was turning to leave when Peter Pan slapped him in the mouth.

"You faggot motherfucker, you set me up. They'll get me killed," she screamed.

Yuseff didn't respond, he just hesitated and gasped without speaking. He was in deep pain. She had hit him in the same place I had. Yuseff went down on one knee. Al turned to make sure he wasn't reaching for a weapon. This moment gave Peter Pan the diversion she needed. Like a flash, she bolted up and leaped past Mack heading towards the door. I stepped out and caught her by the waist. She tried to slap at me but I just ducked, spun around, and caught her by the back of her waistband and yanked upwards until she was hanging in midair.

"You motherfucker," she screamed. "Let me go, you'll get me killed."

"Shut up all that damn noise," Mack said. We're the police, we're here to help you, fool."

She continued kicking until I twisted the waistband so tight that I had cut off her air supply.

"Just calm down, we're here to protect you, you'll be all right."

"Yuseff, you motherfucker, I'm going to get you if it's the last thing I ever do," she bawled as Yuseff exited the Laundromat with tears in his eyes, still holding his bleeding mouth.

Mack signaled his backup who immediately pulled up outside in front of the door. With Mack on one side, and me on the other, we marched Peter Pan out and put her into the waiting car.

"Let's get her out of here," Mack told his backup while he and I climbed into our cars.

Peter Pan was livid, and still cursing.

"This is a violation of my fucking rights. I'm supposed to be able to call a lawyer."

"You ain't under arrest, baby, all we want to do is talk to you, we trying to help you," Mack said.

"You want to get me fuckin killed is what you're trying to do."

"Okay, let her go Mack," I said.

Mack glanced over at me, confused.

"She wants to go, let her go. Within fifteen minutes we'll put the word on the street that she has been in here talking about what she saw at the Tease Me Club and then offer a five hundred dollar reward for her whereabouts, and guaranteed whoever wants you will get to you within twenty-four hours."

Peter Pan was suddenly speechless and deflated.

"She wants to go, let her go. Okay, you're free to go."

Mack had relaxed, seeing what my strategy was. Peter Pan's face dropped, defeated.

"Okay, what you want to know?" she said in a quiet little voice. "That's some dirty shit y'all pulling, I swear."

All the brashness had evaporated. In its place was the shy little boy-looking young woman who had probably once been a little piece of heaven in her father's eyes. In order to keep her from lying we told her what we already knew about her. We told her what we knew about the cocaine orgy, about how she had worked as a hooker for Beresford, and about how she had sold drugs for Yuseff. We also told her that we were not looking to bust her on any of these things. But that we just wanted two things: One, to get all the facts about what happened at The Tease Me Club last Wednesday night; and Two, to keep her from getting killed.

We drove back to the Be-Bop and she told us about the party and how two Asian men busted in and told China Blue she was a traitor then stabbed her. Then she told us about the fight and about how she survived by hiding in the closet. But before she could get to the last part she broke down crying.

"Why you crying, baby?" Mack asked

"'Cause I'm scared if I say anything he'll kill me."

"He who?" Mack wanted to know.

"I don't know his name," she bawled.

"Tell us about him," I coaxed. "Everything you can remember."

"He's crazy," she said.

We got Peter Pan set up with a fat corned beef sandwich and a soda. After she had eaten she settled down enough to tell us about the man who had gone on a killing spree at the orgy. A man who, she said, had stabbed the big Asian man and then started laughing like he had lost his mind.

"Describe him," Mack said.

She looked at me. "He was about as tall as you."

"Dark or light skinned?" I asked.

"Medium brown," she said drinking the soda and searching her memory for details. "And I remember that he had lots of muscles."

"Like he worked out?" I asked.

"Naw, not like Yuseff, like they was more natural, more like, I can't explain it."

"And what else, any scar or anything that stood out?"

She hesitated a moment. "Just," she paused.

"Just what?" Mack asked gently and offered her a chocolate bar from his jacket pocket which she took and began unwrapping.

Mack had a great way with people. He had a softness in his personality that reached out and came through to people in the harshest of times. He made people want to talk to him.

"Just his face. He didn't have no expression. His eyes . . . Like they . . ." she struggled to find the right words. "Like he didn't have no expression in his eyes, in his whole face really, like he didn't never smile, like he couldn't smile or something, but mainly his eyes, like they was messed up or dead or something. I can't explain it, other than he was weird, like, you know, creepy."

"What we are going to do," Mack explained, "is to get one of our artists over here with this special computer and see if we can come up with what he looks like. Okay?"

She nodded her head.

An hour later a female artist showed up with a computerized identification kit that could create a composite face from a data base of noses, lips, facial structures, eyebrows, foreheads, and eyes.

Within an hour we had a photograph of the man we were looking for. Then we arranged for Peter Pan to stay at Mack's place until we could find a safe house.

By then it was the early afternoon. I went back to the bar. There was a message and a fax from Jim Frazier. The subject was Katsu Yamaguchi, Japanese attaché to the U.S. commerce division. Forty-two years old. Born in Osaka, Japan. Educated at Yale and New York University. From a prestigious banking family, trained as a banker. His specialty, financing of international real estate through investment bank financing. He had successfully participated in purchasing, on behalf of Japanese real estate syndicates, over four hundred properties in the U.S. during the past three years. Yamaguchi spoke fluent Japanese, Russian, and English. Single, never married. He was known to have regularly frequented prostitutes, preferred blond women. His hobbies were golf and polo. He was a collector of African American soul music. Drank socially. Not a known drug user.

The background check gave me more than enough to start with. I figured now I had the ammunition I needed to pay his embassy a visit. I called and left Jim a message on his home answering machine, thanking him in code.

The Japanese embassy was located at 229 Park Avenue. It took me thirty minutes by train from Harlem. I mentioned Yamaguchi's name and was able to get an appointment with a Mr. Sumiko, the head of Yamaguchi's department. Sumiko was in his mid fifties and chain-smoked.

"We believe that Mr. Yamaguchi may have been meeting with some business associates when he was killed. Of course the circumstances under which he was killed were somewhat embarrassing and as you can understand, we haven't spoken of this publicly. Of course nothing can be said to the press," Sumiko insisted. "This could be a very touchy subject for our government."

"I understand."

It had never been articulated but the whole reason I had been asked to get involved and find out the truth was to cover political asses in the U.S. as well as in Japan. It was easier to create the perfect lie when one understood the truth.

"What about his family, do they know about his death yet?"

"Nobody from our side except myself and our director know about his death at this stage. We have told all inquires that Mr. Yamaguchi has been sent away on a trip to Russia."

"What about when he eventually doesn't show up?" I asked knowing almost to the word what his answer would be.

"When the time comes, we have made arrangements for a regrettable accident that will not cause embarrassment for our government," the diplomat explained.

"I understand," I said politely. And I did. In the CIA, I had learned that many things reported to the press are not at all as they really happened. A team of specialists are often dispatched to troubleshoot and handle the gory details in cases where incidents might cause political embarrassment or fallout to important individuals or governments. Their job is to create a scenario that fits in with what the public can swallow. I, in fact, had been a part of such teams. By the time the news has been distributed to the media, cover stories have been arranged, and most of the mopping up would have already taken place.

"Was he involved in any business dealings in Harlem?" I asked.

"No, not to my knowledge."

"Could I look through his papers, perhaps there is something that might help me, something only I would recognize?"

"No, Mr. Barnett," Sumiko said, with the practiced smile of a lying diplomat. "I have been over all of Katsu's papers personally and, I assure you, there is nothing there and definitely no business interests in Harlem."

"Okay Mr. Sumiko, thanks for your time."

As sure as my name was Devil Barnett, I knew he was lying. Which made finding out all the more important. I had an idea. I called Mack on my cell phone and asked him to meet me down at the Japanese embassy. Mack arrived with a turkey sandwich for me and two chicken sandwiches for himself. I outlined my plan and told him what I had found out as we ate.

We had about an hour to kill, which we did by swapping funny stories and girl watching.

It was five o'clock before the lady I wanted to see showed up on the sidewalk.

When I recognized her, I walked over and asked for directions to the nearest subway. I stalled some more by pretending to fumble through a tourist map then asked for directions and the best mode of transport to the airport. Afterwards, I returned to the car where Mack was waiting.

"Did you get it?" I asked him.

"Mack nodded smiling, "Got it."

I smiled satisfactorily and jumped into the car.

I knew Sumiko was lying and I felt Billy Lee was telling the truth. Funny thing was, both roads pointed in the same direction. Harlem.

Al and I spent the next morning at The Tease trying to pick up some more clues. We talked around to some of the locals, but nobody seemed to know anything, or at least they weren't telling if they did. A lot of Harlem residents had long ago adopted an attitude of keeping their noses out of other peoples business. It made a lot of sense and, in a place like Harlem, that kind of thinking more often than not was the best kind of life insurance policy. I quizzed Melvin again, but he hadn't heard anything new.

Al Mack and I walked the distance from The Tease at 125th and Lenox back to my place at 126th near 5th Ave. On the way back we sidestepped kids playing, a one-man blues band, and a few sidewalk vendors who had refused to leave the neighborhood despite the fact that the police had banned them along Harlem's main drag.

"There's more to this than meets the eye," I said.

"How do you mean?"

"The most obvious thing that keeps popping up is the drug connection. And when all roads lead to the obvious, my nose tells me that nine times out of ten, the obvious answer is not the right answer."

"I'll go with your nose," Mack chuckled.

We walked for the next few minutes in silence mulling over the facts in our minds.

"I'll catch up with you, got to put in my number," Mack told me as we approached the corner of 126th. "Set me up a ham on rye with mustard, I could eat a bear."

"Cool."

He ducked into Walcott's barbershop to place his bet and I headed in to work.

I still had not been able to find that damn warranty card for the new refrigerator, and it was driving me crazy. If I didn't find it, I would have to pay a service charge, which I did not want to do. The service charge alone would be the cost of getting a used refrigerator unit. I needed to find that damned card.

As I entered the Be-Bop, two men standing inside turned to greet me. Asians. The younger one was in his late twenties, about five foot seven wearing a close cropped haircut, a black leather jacket, and dark shades. He was built like a weight lifter. The other man looked to be in his early forties, shorter, well-dressed, and wearing gold-rimmed eyeglasses.

"Mr. Barnett," the well-dressed man spoke up.

"Yes."

"My name is John Soo. I represent the Sun Bright Realty company," he said extending his business card toward me.

I took it and glanced at it. Expensively done.

"If you have a few moments," he continued, "I would like to speak with you."

I walked to a place at the end of the bar and took a seat. Mr. Soo took the stool directly to the right of me; the weight lifter took the stool to the left.

"What will you have?" I asked Soo.

"Just coffee for me thank you," Mr. Soo said.

The younger man declined my hospitality.

I gave Duke the order for two coffees and also put in for Mack's sandwich.

"Mind if I smoke, nasty habit," Soo apologized through an expensive set of dental work.

"Be my guest."

Duke brought the coffee as Soo lit up a French Gauloises cigarette he carried in an expensive looking silver cigarette case.

"To get right down to business, my company has gotten word that you've been making a number of inquiries into our activities here in Harlem."

"Is that a bad thing?"

"No, not necessarily, but as you already know two of our employees were recently killed and we are very interested in evidence leading to the circumstances surrounding their deaths."

"And you came to see me because . . ." I let the rest of the sentence hang in midair.

"Well," Soo inhaled deeply and blew the smoke in the opposite direction over his shoulder. "We hoped that you might be able and willing to share your findings with us."

"I see."

"Does that sound like an interesting proposition for you? We would pay for that information. Say, at the rate of four hundred per day, plus expenses for a guaranteed number of days, say two weeks."

Our drinks arrived.

I calculated in my head. Fifty six hundred dollars for two weeks work. That meant they had already tried to come up with some answers and had drawn a blank. Now they needed someone who knew how to decipher and interpret the sounds and meanings of events in the Harlem jungle. Either that or they knew something already that I was sure to eventually find out, in which case the fifty six hundred was pure and simple hush mouth money.

Either way the offer didn't appeal to me.

"Sorry Mr. Soo," I began sipping the hot coffee, "but I have one client that I am working for exclusively."

"I'm sorry to hear that," the well dressed Asian said inhaling from his cigarette again.

"The way of the world, I suppose."

Soo lapsed into silence for a moment and I could almost see the wheels turning in his brain. He was figuring his next best move. But since they had come fishing in my pond, I decided that I would do some fishing of my own, only I would use my own kind of bait.

I broke the silence.

"Could it be that Sun Bright Realty is so interested in what I might find out because it could lead to an interruption of the profits pouring in from those fruit and vegetable stands you guys finance up in Harlem?"

Soo stiffened and took a deep breath. The younger Korean turned his attention toward me. I had struck a deep nerve. My Harlem bait had caught a Korean fish.

"We do have varied interests in Harlem as well as all over the city, Mr. Barnett, however I will admit that certain information you could turn up may have an outcome on future business."

This sophisticated Asian was very cagey. He was coolly trying to double talk me, but he was still on my hook. So I decided I'd take him into deeper waters.

"From my understanding, the Kim brothers were enforcers who collected for an extortion racket that you guys run among Asian business all over Harlem."

Soo's jaw tightened as he stubbed out his smoke.

"Mr. Barnett," he said softly, fighting to keep his cool, "I did not come here to insult you, so why do you insult me? Sun Bright Realty is legitimate in every way, I can assure you."

"I never said it wasn't."

"Exactly what are you saying then?"

"I'm just telling you what the word on the street is, and I'm giving you that one for free," I quipped as I continued sipping my coffee.

"If it's a matter of price, I can go up to five hundred per day," Soo offered.

"Mr. Soo, I appreciate your offer, however I usually only work for people who I either respect or like and, to be honest, Sun Bright Realty doesn't fall into either of those categories."

Anger surged up in Soo's dark eyes as the younger man shifted his weight onto the foot nearest me.

"Mr. Soo does not like to be insulted," the younger muscled Korean said with a thick accent as he banged his meaty fist angrily on the counter.

Duke looked up at the sound. Soo glared at the younger man and spat some angry word in Korean in his direction. The muscleman responded in Korean, and bowed obsequiously in Soo's direction.

Obviously he was supposed to be seen and not heard.

Slowly Duke began moving towards the cash register, easing his hand under the counter where I kept a loaded sawed off shotgun.

"Mr.," the booming sound came from behind us drawing our attention. The voice belonged to Al Mack who was standing in the doorway and looking at the three of us seated near the end of the bar. Mack was pointing his huge finger at the younger man.

"Have you ever seen an oriental man walking down a Harlem street with a pair of twelves sticking out of his ass?" Al moved his sportcoat back to reveal his revolver holstered to his ample waist.

I smiled in Soo's direction.

"Well, the man asked a question," I said turning in the younger man's direction. If I had moved an inch closer the angry fire in the muscular Korean's eyes would have scorched me.

Soo stood up and started to walk out but Mack was still blocking the door.

I nodded and Mack moved to the side to let them pass.

Soo paused and turned towards me.

"Our business is not yet finished, Mr. Barnett. We will meet again, you can count on it," he said then left.

His veiled threat had registered, but so what? I had been threatened more times than I had fingers and toes and I was still alive to tell the tale.

"What was that all about?" Mack wanted to know.

"Just the rats coming out of hiding."

"That means we must be getting closer to something, even closer than we realize. You can bet it's a lot closer than someone is comfortable with, otherwise they would still be laying back in the cut," Mack mused.

"Prezackly," I grinned.

I called Uncle Beans' office knowing that he usually worked late. I needed to fill him in as well as ask his advice on a few things. To my surprise Kit answered.

"What are you doing there?"

"Working on preparing my presentation for the DA's interview and, let me tell you, it ain't no play thang," she said.

"I can imagine. I had hoped to catch up with Uncle Beans."

"He left early today, that damn stomach trouble again. He left a message for you to try him at home. If you don't get him, call him at Barbara's place."

She gave me Barbara's number.

"Think we can find a way to get him checked out?" I asked.

"I was just thinking about that myself, but I'm at a loss."

"If he goes in now maybe that can stop whatever it is causing it, before it gets worse."

"I think he's scared myself," Kit said.

"Uncle Beans, scared of going to the doctor. The image somehow doesn't quite fit, " I said.

"You know Mommy died of cancer, maybe he's afraid he's got it too."

I reflected on her words. Maybe Kit was right. I had known killers who were afraid to go to the dentist and take a needle in the gums, yet the same person would commit cold blooded mass murder without a second thought.

"Miss Pritchard says she's going to make him up one of her special homemade remedies to help his stomach. If that doesn't work, we'll find a way to get him to the doctor's even if we have to tie him." Kit said.

"Just let me know, I'll bring the rope."

She laughed and I hung up.

Just the thought of Uncle Beans being ill grated against my psyche. With Dad having recently died I was not ready to face another emotional loss. I guess nobody ever really is.

From the back of the bar, where my office was located, I could hear sounds of laughter like the people up front were having a party. I walked out to get a closer look and came upon Diego McMichael, an old friend of Dad's who I hadn't seen since the funeral. He was at the bar talking loud and drawing a crowd. Clowning, laughing, drinking, and telling lies, as usual, he had everybody laughing fit to burst at the seams. Johnny Boy, one of the regulars whose stock and trade was bumming drinks, walked over to where Diego had the crowd going.

"Hey D., where you been?" Johnny Boy asked, looking Diego over and sizing him up to bum a drink.

Diego was dressed sharply in a double-breasted black and gray checked suit with a sky blue shirt and a silk tie. On his feet he wore expensive Italian loafers and on his head sat a beaver skin wide brim hat. As the saying goes, he was as sharp as rat shit, and that's sharp on both ends. He always dressed well. It was his trademark.

"Taking care of my business," Diego told him.

"Listen, you looking prosperous, buy your old buddy a beer. Better still, loan me five bucks."

Diego leaned back on the stool and gave him a long hard look.

"Listen, Johnny Boy, I want to tell you something and I want everybody to hear this. Hey y'all," Diego called out to the entire room. "This man here just asked me to loan him some of my hard earned social security check. The man knows I'm retired and he's young and strong, still he asked me for my little social security money to buy him a drink, but I'm going to tell him this, I want all y'all to be a witness . . ."

Ears collectively perked up. Diego was setting Johnny Boy up for the big fall. Smiles came out on everyone's faces and they tuned in and hung on every word.

Diego began:

> A friend ain't shit,
> I met an old pal who I treated so fine
> Bought him corn whiskey, champagne, and wine.
> But when I fell, I fell so low.
> Didn't have no friends and nowhere to go.
> And I said to my old friend, I said please loan me one dime.
> And this is what he said to me. He said . . .
> You have to be blind and cannot see
> Both legs cut off, up above your knee.
> Have the tuberculosis and the German Flu
> With lice around your collar singing Doodley Do.
> Have the Mexican measles and the Boston hiccups.
> You can bring me the Atlantic in the smallest teacup.
> Then bring the blood off the rock that killed Goliath,
> And the three Hebrew chillun from the burning fire.
> Bring the king who delivered Daniel from the lions den,
> And four or five of Pharaoh's men.
> Not only that, but your mother has to come screaming and
> crying
> With a letter in her hand saying son, you're grandma's dying.
> That's the fix in which you have to be.
> Before you can get one dime from me.

The crowd burst into applause and laughter rang out as if the bar was a performing theatre. Diego, who loved every minute of it, actually turned and tipped his hat to the crowd. Johnny Boy laughed so hard that tears ran down his face.

"That one deserves a drink on the house," I yelled in his direction.

Diego turned to look at me, still grinning.

"Diego, what you coming in my place and taking over for?"

He hugged me tightly. I laughed and hugged him in return. He was surprisingly strong for a man in his early eighties.

"Man, where you been?" he asked with traces of a Mississippi accent.

"Right here, since the funeral," I said.

"Man, I'm sure glad to see you, you know I've been down south visiting my sister. She was sick, that's why you ain't seen me, but I'm back now," he said as I poured out his regular shot of E&J and a small glass of ginger ale.

"You ain't forgot have you," he grinned, holding up the liquor to the light. "A little shot of Easy Jesus goes a long, long way," he said and swallowed the drink.

We talked about the old days, about the times Diego and Dad and I had gone fishing together and other things that brought back lots of memories. I felt glad about a couple of things. Glad that men like him were still around to share life with. Glad that I was making headway on the murder case.

Later I put in a call to Onion who picked up the phone on the third ring. I told him I was looking for anything on Sun Bright Realty and to cross check to see if they had recently filed any change of deeds notices or had any business dealings in Harlem. He said he would. We agreed to talk the next day. Onion was one of a kind. He lived in a two-room apartment in upstate New York with his wife Jesse. Onion, who was confined to a wheelchair, sometimes worked on a freelance basis for the CIA as a researcher. The CIA used a lot of specialists. Onion had been involved in computers since the late sixties as a kid. Simply put, he was a genius. Over the years we had grown to be friends. His real name was Dale Burton, but Jim Frazier and I had pinned him with the nickname Onion over ten years ago, after spending a week with him. We discovered that every meal he ordered or ate had to include onions. He even ate onions with peanut butter and jelly. *Yuck!*

The name stuck. I think he liked it because it gave him a kind of distinction and made him more than just another crippled computer nerd.

I called The Tease Club and asked for Honey Lavelle. Raymond, one of the bartenders, answered. He said she hadn't been in yet, but was expected later.

It was Friday, the start of another weekend and the Be-Bop had started to get busier. The regulars had cashed their checks and had taken their usual places at the bar. A group of office workers were celebrating someone's promotion. One step closer towards the glass ceiling. Christine was taking care of things so well I decided to cool out for a while. Besides my body told me that I needed the rest.

Although it had only been a week and a half, it seemed like a month had passed between last Wednesday and now. I wasn't planning to call my Uncle for a couple hours so I decided to spend the time listening to a new stack of jazz CDs that the juke-box caretaker had left. My collection was all neatly stacked in a holder on my file cabinet. I put the Acoustic Alchemy, George Benson, Basia, and Errol Klugh into the player, kicked my feet up on the desk, and turned off the light.

Dad had named the bar the Be-Bop Tavern because of his love for the music of Bud Powell, Thelonius Monk, Dizzy Gillespie, Miles Davis, and various other bebop jazz musicians who passed through Minton's in the late forties. People who were only into Duke Ellington and Count Basie considered bebop's atonality and fusion of intricate melodies inside the harmonic structure something weird and crazy. They called it Chinese music. When I was a kid, Dad would sometimes take off from the bar and we would go to the jazzmobile, a traveling jazz workshop where the old timers would come to Harlem and show the young kids how to play. This kind of experience was just one of the real beautiful things about growing up in Harlem. A culture that got exported to the world started right here in our own backyard.

Even though their approach to life was different in many ways, both Dad and Uncle Beans had a similar philosophy. They both mixed their knowledge with kindness that ended up as wisdom.

Dad was always open to thinking in a different way, and that rubbed off on me. Maybe that's why I decided to join the Agency when I had been approached. It was something altogether differ-ent from what I had ever considered before. Up until that time Dad, Uncle Beans, and myself always thought I'd most likely be-come a lawyer. Uncle Beans and Dad had it all planned out. I'd be-come a lawyer, then help them build their dreams. On the civil rights side I would fight those cases that were unpopular but mean-ingful, and on the business side I would look over the paperwork of the deals that would put millions in our pockets. When I told them that I really wanted to try a career as an agent in the CIA, at first Uncle Beans offered strong resistance. But Dad explained to him that if I didn't get it out of my system now, no matter how successful I became as a lawyer, I would go through life thinking I'd missed something and hold them responsible. Eventually, Uncle Beans saw the sense of the argument and became one of my strongest supporters. Well, at least now, Uncle Beans had Kit. And I was going to do my part to see that she helped him build his empire and live out his dream.

I was eleven when Mom died from complications resulting from diabetes. Dad sat me down and explained that it wasn't going to be easy and that he wasn't going to be as good as Mom was at most things. But he promised that whatever I was thinking or feeling I could talk to him about it. And over the years he had kept his word. My maternal grandmother moved in a week after my mother's funeral to help raise me. My mother had been her only child. My father prepared the main floor of our house for her and she lived a happy, full life there until she died five years ago. Grandma's name was Sally Henson. She was strong and full of wisdom and old wise sayings. She knew life and loved living it. She loved my Dad and Uncle Beans too, just like they were her own sons. One day when we were talking she told me that Mom had been one of the luckiest women in the world because she had married Dad.

At around nine o'clock I called Uncle Beans' house. He wasn't in, so I used the number for Barbara that Kit had given me. He was there and asked me to come over.

When I arrived at Barbara's house it was almost 10:00 P.M. My uncle was watching the news on TV and drinking a cup of hot milk. He looked alright. I asked him if he was in any pain and he said he was feeling fine.

"I'm being well taken care of," Uncle Beans said, looking in Barbara's direction. "She used to be a nurse."

"He'll be alright, just too much of eating the wrong things, I'm putting him on a diet," Barbara said in her deep velvet voice.

"By any chance can you sing?" I asked her.

"My lord no, I can't carry a tune in a bucket," Barbara laughed. "Everyone asks that when they hear me speak. Even if I could sing I'd be too shy to get up on stage."

When Uncle Beans had finished watching the news, I started to fill him in on Lee's death as well my theory of their being a professional killer involved. Barbara stayed in the room reading a magazine while we talked.

"I think there's a connection somewhere to this Sun Bright Realty," I said.

"I think you might have something," he agreed.

"I'm not saying for sure, I just think there might be a good chance. Why do you say so?"

"One of the Korean guys who was found dead, turns out I knew him. Well, not personally. but I knew of him, let's say."

"How?"

"He was involved with shaking down businesses that were financed by Sun Bright Realty, but they were also involved in shaking down other Koreans who had no connection to Sun Bright. Lee was Korean as you already know but he was doing business outside of their network, and he had been approached by the Sun Bright thug to see if he would be interested in selling his interest in a property that we were involved in, to Sun Bright. If Lee had owned the property by himself, they could have leaned on him, but since he owned it with me they couldn't afford to," my uncle explained.

"You own some property with Koreans, that's a switch. I thought you were a big advocate on keeping Koreans out of Harlem?"

"I'm for keeping exploitation out of Harlem. Lee wasn't for just lining his own pockets. He understood that if he operated here then he had to be willing to pay the piper and give something back, that's why I made him part of the Landmark Development Committee I put together, to make certain buildings in Harlem landmarks."

"Landmarks?"

"Yeah, there's a lot of money in landmarks, tax breaks," he winked.

"How does that work?" I wanted to know.

"When a building is declared a landmark, there can be tax advantages for the companies doing business there, especially if the landmark is declared a non-profit corporation. Lee and I were working on a deal that would be beneficial for those involved in a couple buildings that I'm working to get designated as landmarks. Sun Bright wanted to buy the buildings outright so they could expand their operations. But I told them we wouldn't sell. For the long term, the tax break will be more lucrative. If you have an office space in a landmark, not only are your operating expenses immediately cut, you can create all kinds of other deals around it. The buildings may be raggedy, but you've got to remember, Harlem is still in one of the top real estate markets in the world. Land in Harlem can still be worth big bucks."

Barbara went to the kitchen and came out with a fresh cup of warm milk and sat it on the table next to my uncle.

"Barbara, listen to this, Lee was found murdered. Him and his daughter," Uncle Beans told her.

"Yes, Korean Lee who serves on the Landmark Committee with us."

"My Lord, when?" she asked.

"This morning, right?" he turned to me.

"Yes, that's when they found him."

"My lord," Barbara repeated. "I was just, just talking to him last week. What a shame. Anybody know how it happened, or who did it?" she asked.

"Not sure yet," my uncle answered.

"If it ain't one thing it's another," Barbara said, shaking her head solemnly. Then she turned to me. "Would you like something to drink?"

"No, I'm fine. I just wanted to bring my uncle up to date, I'm heading home."

"Okay, I'll see you later," Barbara said and left the room.

She was wearing a silk dress that wrapped closely around her trim figure. I saw clearly for the first time what had been keeping my uncle occupied, even why he agreed to marry her. Barbara

Simmons had the kind of body that would make a man glad to come home at night.

At 12:02 A.M. I arrived home. At 12:06 A.M. the telephone rang. It was Honey Lavelle on the other end.

"Youngblood, I heard you called looking for me. If it's what I'm hoping you called for, tonight won't be a good night for it. I've had one helluva day."

"What did you think I called for?"

"You tell me . . ."

"I need a favor."

"What did you have in mind?"

"I'd rather not discuss it on the phone."

Silence on the other end was then followed by Honey's laughter.

"You know, I must be getting old. I'm letting a Youngbbood like you set me up."

"What are you talking about," I said innocently.

"What am I talking about? Okay, okay you got me interested. So what's the deal? Come on tell me."

"I need a place for a young lady to stay for a few days until I can work out some things. Her life may be in danger. I'll explain in more detail when I see you."

"When do you need it?"

"ASAP. But nobody can know about this."

"Okay, call me in the morning after nine, I'll have something for you."

"Just like that, huh?"

"Listen Youngblood, if you didn't think I could deliver, you wouldn't have called, so don't try to act impressed. You set me up good one time, but don't push your luck. Okay?"

"Okay."

"In the morning then," Honey said, and hung up.

I climbed into bed a few minutes later and lay quiet for a long time thinking, just thinking. I thought about the pieces of this puzzle that I was starting to see fit together. I thought about Honey Lavelle and her soft pink lipstick that matched her nail polish. I liked Honey, and thought about maybe I would get the chance to take her up on her offer if it was still good. One day soon, just maybe.

As I lay thinking a sharp pain shot through my body, then subsided. It was then that I realized just how tired I really was. In fact, I was beat down to my socks. My back was aching at a place I didn't even want to think about. Way back deep in my bones where the pain associated with my dreaded disease emanated from. I needed rest, a long rest. I guess the stress of running the bar and being constantly on the go without much sleep over the past week was finally catching up with me. I wanted to drop right off to sleep but my nerve endings were still doing the tango to the tune of, Who killed Who and Why. The pieces of the puzzle turned over and over again and again in my mind.

I got up and peered out of the window at the night sky. The ceiling of the world appeared deep, dark, and rich tonight like a black velvet cover. The moon peeped out sheepishly from behind passing clouds and the wind lifted the smell of fresh rain and carried it straight into my brain giving me a rush of adrenaline. I sat down in a nearby chair and turned my mind to what I could eat when the phone rang.

Maxine's voice was at the other end.

"Hey baby," she purred.

"Hey yourself, I thought you would be recovering."

"A woman's work is never done, you know that."

"In your case, make that two women," I said, alluding to the endless string of men who always seemed to be infatuated by her.

She laughed good-naturedly.

"I just called to say thank you for showing up for Hamp's birthday party."

"Wouldn't have missed it for the world. Did Hamp like the gift?"

"Had to make him put that darn Nintendo down. He took it to bed with him."

"Glad he liked it."

"You sound whipped."

"I am."

"What, pussy whipped?" she quipped mischievously.

"I wish," was my honest reply.

"Speaking of which," she said, "Sonia was quite impressed by you."

"Really?" My interest perked up a bit.

"Really, she asked me who you were and what you were really about."

"What did you say?"

"I told her the truth, I said you were a homosexual, and if your boyfriend caught her talking to you he would scratch her eyes out."

"Oh no, you didn't."

Maxine's raucous laughter filled the phone. When she finally stopped she said, "No, I didn't. I told her you were a first class brotha, and that she was very lucky that you were interested in her."

"Thank you."

"Well, it's the truth. I do manage honesty sometimes you know."

I laughed. Maxine was truly one of a kind.

"Guess what," she continued. "I'm in therapy."

"Therapy, for what?"

"Jealousy, I'm dealing with my jealousy on a professional level."

"Jealousy, huh?"

"Yeah, the therapist is helping me not to be jealous of my boyfriends."

"Maxine, the thing I never understood, was that for as long as I've know you, you've always dated more than one guy at a time and yet you are the one who's always jealous. They should be the jealous ones."

"I don't like jealous men. If I find out they're the jealous type, I drop them."

"I can't figure it," I admitted.

"Well, I couldn't either dear, that's why I'm in therapy."

"Is it helping?"

"Don't know. It's all women and we get together and talk about all the shit men put us through."

"Oh yeah. Maxine, I've known you for nineteen years, and if I know you for one hundred and nineteen more, I still won't understand you."

"You understand me better than you know you do, that's why we have stayed friends all these years, Devil. You accept me for who I am."

"Well I like who you are, what else am I suppose to do?"

There was a moment of silence.

"Listen man, don't be getting all deep on me and making me think," she said her voice rising in pitch.

Maxine had a funny way of rushing on to the next thing or changing the subject when she felt real emotion, or something that you said touched her deeply. She was very sensitive but didn't like showing it.

"I'm not getting deep."

"Listen, I just called to thank you again for coming. I love you and Hamp loves you."

She blew a kiss down the line then hung up.

I smiled at myself. Maxine was one of a kind, in a category all by herself. Sometimes she was as cool and confident as a relaxing tiger, and other times as vulnerable and sensitive as a newborn kitten. Strange, yet very loving and honest. She had tremendous courage, which I loved her for. I was glad that she was a friend and a part of my life and I was especially glad she allowed me to be a part of Hamp's life.

The thought of Maxine led me to thinking about Sonia and then Amanda. No matter where I turned the road somehow always led back to Amanda. Maybe she was the only one I had ever really loved. I couldn't be sure and, maybe, I would never know. I did know however, that she would always be a part of me, a part I would never be able to leave behind.

Suddenly I felt more tired than ever.

I had discovered over the years, from dealing with my illness, that there is probably no worse physical feeling than when your own body turns against you, when every nerve ending launches a terrorist attack against its host. I had been extremely lucky. In the past fifteen years, I had only had three serious sickle cell crisis attacks.

The first time I was able to recover at home, but the other two sent me to the hospital. The first hospitalization period came after I had performed my first wet assignment for the Agency. I had emptied a .45 automatic into the face of a man who had been responsible for the killing of five CIA agents. I had never shot anyone before. The mental and emotional stress made something inside of me snap. Despite my training, I found that killing another human being still went against everything I had ever been taught. I had to train myself to accept assassination both on an intellectual and emotional level, otherwise I would not have been able to survive either the job or the demons that would have eventually taken over my mind.

The second time I was hospitalized was when my grandmother died. The day I received the news, I walked more than five miles in the blistering cold thinking about what she had meant to me, not realizing that the cold and the emotional stress together could combine to bring on an attack.

I remember once when I was about fourteen and suffering back pains as a result of the disease, my grandmother was treating me with heating pads and liniment rubs. She told me that my illness was just a condition of life that must be lived with as naturally as possible in the same way as if someone had one leg shorter than the other or a humped back.

She often talked about a place inside your soul where you could go to get a deep inner strength supplied by God that would carry a person through all kinds of problems and bring them out on the other side.

Many sicklers never even make it into adulthood but others like me lead relatively normal lives. Still, at any moment an attack can take place and I will be at the mercy of the kind of excruciating pain that doctors have measured as being nine times more intensive than the pain a woman experiences in childbirth. Doctors control this pain with highly addictive drugs (usually dyhydracodiene or dyamorphine, which is actually heroin). I live in fear of these drugs more than the pain because I have known people who became junkies from their bouts with sickle cell.

My grandmother had been a volunteer worker in a veteran's hospital during World War II and she had seen first hand how medicine given to patients for pain turned them into junkies. To her, it was all the same, whether you were lying in a hospital bed or standing in a deep nod on 125th Street, a junkie was a junkie; and if she had anything to do with it, her grandson was not about to be added to the statistics of dope addicts in Harlem. Through my grandmother, I was introduced to Dr. Fola OgunBayo, a Nigerian healer. Dr. OgunBayo had treated thousands of sickle cell patients in West Africa with herbs. Dr. OgunBayo began by giving me chewing sticks from a Nigerian tree that he said would help my blood to flow as smooth as a river. So, for many years, I have chewed sticks from the tree that botanists have labelled the Oriata Fagura, along with a diet that includes cassava, fresh fruits, lots of water, vegetables, and regular yoga and Tai Chi exercises. All combine to help keep my killer disease under control. I remember reading somewhere once that there had even been research done in the U.S. with the bark from the Oriata Fagura, but the researchers failed to get FDA approval. Not surprising if you consider that the major drug companies have a lot more to gain from selling synthetic codeine and morphine already in stock than by developing a drug from a tree in some Nigerian forest.

I know that a major part of me still resists drug treatment because of my grandmother's point of view. And also because in some strange way, I believe that I'm still connected to her strength and spirit and I will be able to withstand and overcome the pain.

And though I walked without fear of falling, my ultimate tumble still lurked dangerously and silently in the shadows. Because I had the sickle cell disease, my life in many ways has always been like a ticking bomb. I guess one option would have been to become cautious and live a life dictated by the constraints of the disease. But I just wasn't built that way. I decided I was no better or worse off than anyone else. Maybe that's another reason why I came back to Harlem. There were things here that I had grown up with, things that I needed to be a part of. Even if it meant facing those fears I had developed surrounding my disease. Foremost was the fear that passing the disease to my children may have stopped me

from getting married and starting my own family. Even my pho-
bias had their roots here in Harlem. All of that was part of me, and
I was part of it. Maybe it was a kind of dysfunctional love everlast-
ing. Who knows. Anyway the only thing that really mattered now
was that I needed Harlem to sustain that something in me that
fought ceaselessly to stay alive. And now, Harlem also needed me.

Saturday, 8:30 A.M.
■ Sugar Hill, Harlem

I woke up sweating from a nightmare. I'd been dreaming about Amanda. It was a recurring dream. When I first lost her the dream was frequent. But as time passed, I dreamt it less. Amanda was lying dead among twenty or so other bodies with a bullet in her head. And as I looked down at her, she opened her eyes and looked up at me. I could hear her voice saying, "Why did you sell me out my love? Why did you do it?" I felt shaken.

I got up and took a hot shower hoping that it would wash away some of the memories. Amanda was dead and that was that. It had been two years, but sometimes it seemed that I could hear her gentle voice laughing in the wind. That's what love will do to you, I guess.

I was having coffee when the phone rang. It was Mack.

"Hey, what are you doing bugging me so early on a Saturday?" I said good-naturedly.

"Early, man half the day is gone. You know as well as I do, ain't no rest for the wicked," he shot back, "Get on up and I'll meet you at your place, I've got copies of the sketch."

"How did our girl sleep last night?"

Neither Mack or myself trusted anyone at the police station with where Peter Pan was staying. Mack was even more aware than I was about the network of corruption that ran rampant through the NYPD ranks. He said that there were guys in the department who would sell Jesus Christ out for a pack of smokes. And I believed him.

"Man, I've never seen anybody so small eat so much," Mack laughed. "But she's cool. Sleeping. My wife is staying home to make sure she don't suddenly get a case of the itchy feet."

"Good. Give me thirty minutes and I'll meet you at the bar."

"Okay, in a minute," Mack said and hung up.

I listened to my *Fourplay* CD as I drove down to the Be-Bop. Mack was already there when I arrived, engrossed in conversation with Christine.

"Superstition is something people won't ever give up. And on the first day of the New Year, if it's a woman that comes to my mother's house, my mother will tell her to go home and come back later. It has to be a man that comes in the house first on New Year's Day, otherwise it brings bad luck," Mack winked and smiled.

"What about hats on the bed?" I joined in the conversation. "My grandmother thought it brought bad luck if a man puts his hat on the bed. Had to put hats on the chair in my grandmother's house."

"Mine too," Mack grinned.

The sketch that Mack had brought showed a middle-aged black man in his late thirties to early forties. He had a thin hard face with cheeks that sunk in. His eyes were dark and distant in their deep-set hollow sockets.

"We're circulating this throughout Harlem along with a cash reward, no questions asked. That should get the fat frying," Mack said. "Anything new on the real estate angle?"

"Yeah, I learned some things from my uncle last night."

I recapped the conversation from the night before with Uncle Beans while Mack sat listening and sipping a cup of coffee.

"Yeah, yeah," was all he said after I had finished.

I looked at my watch. It was almost 10:00 A.M. I went back to my office and phoned Honey Lavelle.

"Thought you had forgotten about me, Youngbbood," she said in a sleepy voice. "It's all arranged. She can stay at my place. It's safe. I live alone."

"Good, I'll call you back this afternoon and set a time to bring her over."

"Today is my off day, so anytime is good."

When I returned to the booth, Mack was having another coffee.

"Those photographs from yesterday. Let's go get them."

"Okay, let's go then," Mack said finishing off the coffee and rising from the booth.

We drove south and stopped at Gorman's Fast and Easy Photo Shop along the way.

Twenty minutes later, Mack pulled up in front of the Japanese embassy and I jumped out and went in. I rode the elevator up to the office occupied by Miss Oguni, who was secretary to Mr. Suntiko. Mack waited around the corner. I returned to the car five minutes later.

"How did it go?" Mack asked me.

"Like a dream, but we'll know more in just about an hour."

It was noon. We ate lunch to kill some time. At 1:01 P.M. precisely, Miss Oguni came out of the Japanese embassy and walked to the corner. She went into the Kentucky Fried Chicken carry out located in the middle of the block, ordered a tea to stay, and sat down. A few moments later, I joined her.

"Good afternoon."

She didn't speak. She only returned my look with tears in her eyes. Underneath the tears were hatred and fear. She placed a nine by twelve envelope onto the seat next to her and looked down into her cup. I took the envelope and calmly walked out and down the block to Mack waiting in the sedan.

"Okay?"

"Okay," I confirmed.

"Man you are something else," Mack grinned as we headed north, back towards Harlem.

Inside the envelope was the appointment book of one Mr. Katsu Yamaguchi. In order to get it, I had had to stage the kind of incident that I had carried out with regularity when I had worked as an operative in the CIA. Blackmail. Put it this way, Miss Oguni had been framed. Mack had taken snapshots of her talking to one Marcus Barnett, an ex-agent of the CIA. Photographs that could be misconstrued by the Japanese government, which would bring shame not only to Miss Oguni, but to her family in Japan as well.

Basic training in any governmental intelligence agency teaches that results are more important that any moral considerations. Morality is a luxury that CIA operatives do not allow themselves or others. A code of immorality governs the nature of all counter intelligence. Miss Oguni was a mere pawn in the game.

Onion called at 2:45 P.M. to inform me about what he had found out on Sun Bright Realty. He said that Sun Bright Realty had been purchasing lots of real estate in Harlem over the past year. According to their tax records, they had paid out five grand to a Setsuko Nakamora for consulting fees. Where and how Onion got his information was always a mystery to me. IRS records, private corporate records, account files — you name it, Onion had or could get access to it. The NYPD was picking up my expenses so I asked him to bill me at double the rate. I thanked him and told him I wasn't finished with him yet.

"How about some tickets to the Knicks game, they're sizzling? Think of it as a bonus," Onion suggested. He was a huge basketball fan and for the first time in five years the New York Knicks were in first place.

"Hold tight, I'll check on it," I told him and hung up.

In Yamaguchi's appointment book, there was an entry made thirteen days before his death: *Setsuko Nakamora., pay $6K corn. via Oni.* At least it confirmed what I had been thinking. That Setsuko Nakamora, aka China Blue, had been working for the Koreans and was working with Yamaguchi also.

I put in a call to Christine at the Be-Bop.

"Hey, when do you want to see the new ideas for the remodeling I came up with?" Christine asked when she came on the line, which broke my train of thought.

"What?"

"The plans, Devil. You said earlier that you wanted to hear my plans, or did you change your mind about me being the manager," she asked.

"No, everything's cool. I just had my mind on something else. We'll talk about the plans whenever you want."

"But you're always so busy. I need your undivided attention for a couple hours, that's all."

"You're right. Why don't we pick one evening when Duke is on the night shift and meet over at my place, I'll cook dinner for you and we can go over your plans."

"You think I trust you enough to let you cook for me, after I've seen what you can do to a hamburger," she laughed.

I laughed too. I had to admit, I was a lousy cook.

"No, tell you what, I'll cook the dinner, you just study the plans," she said.

"You got a deal," I laughed.

Christine had been a godsend. Over the months she had worked for me we had grown close. She was a straight-up person and to her credit always did her best and kept her word. That she could read my moods also helped. For Christine, as with many young women born and raised in Harlem, life had not been too kind. I promised to myself that I would do my best to give her the break she needed and deserved.

Mack and I arrived at Honey's place with Peter Pan at about 9:00 P.M. Honey had cooked up some chicken wings and had opened a bottle of wine. We ate and talked about security arrangements. Honey had a two-bedroom apartment. One bedroom she used for herself and the other she used for her son when he came to town. Honey said that she would take off the next week from work, so that she could stand guard over our prize.

Honey and Peter Pan seemed to get along from the beginning. Honey had a way of feeling a person out and letting them know she understood where they were coming from. I still had some questions for Peter Pan.

"How did you get on to Yamaguchi?"

"China Blue, I told you before."

"Did he know that it was China who set it up?"

"I don't know. I hit on him just like China told me to after she spoke to the man on the phone. I picked him up at the UN and brought him to the party," Peter Pan explained very matter of factly. "I think she was doing what the man on the phone was telling her to."

"The man on the phone? What man on the phone?" This was the first time she had mentioned it.

"Some man on the phone China was talking to when I was over there to get the Japanese guy's picture so I would know what he looked like.

"Okaay," Mack and I traded looks. Mack talked to her using his most soothing approach.

"Okay baby, now just take your time and tell us everything about this man on the phone," Mack said and congenially offered Peter Pan another soda. He knew she liked soda. This was where Mack shined. I sat back and watched him use his non-threatening persona to get a story from her without any pressure. When Mack turned on the charm he had a way of making even a smart ass, tough street type petty criminal like Peter Pan want to talk.

"I was at chilling at China's place when he called. She was in the bathroom when he called," Peter Pan continued. "And he started asking questions about who I was and what I was doing there. I told him to mind his own business, then went and called China. China got really agitated talking to him. They was talking about bringing Yamaguchi to the party, I think."

Peter Pan yawned and suggested that she might be able to re-member more after she slept some more.

"Last night was the first good sleep I had in a week" she told us. With that, she retired for the night.

"So," I said looking at Mack.

"Like we said before, the minute you think you got one thing nailed down, then here comes some other shit, that's Harlem." Mack shrugged his big shoulders.

"Where the hell do we start looking for a voice on the phone?"

Mack shrugged his shoulders again. "Who knows, we could check all calls to and from China Blue's phone?"

"That won't do us much good if it came from a phone booth."

Mack and I kicked around a few theories while Honey listened attentively but said nothing.

Eventually Mack left for home. Honey and I talked a while and watched an old movie on cable, *It Happened One Night,* starring Clark Gable. I turned to her half in earnest and half in jest because I was feeling the two glasses of wine I had just drunk.

"Thanks for everything, now I guess I owe you." In my head I was half flirting. I'm not sure what the other half of me was doing.

"Maybe I'll consider it a debt paid for what your Dad did for me, maybe I won't. Haven't made up my mind yet," she said.

Honey was originally from Detroit, Michigan, the daughter of a teacher and a bricklayer. She had come to New York seeking fame and fortune as a singer, but got involved with the fast life when she married a would-be record producer who produced more coke and weed sales than he did music. She had been on parade at all of the big fights, parties, and Caribbean cruises because her husband's clientele were mostly in the music or movie industry. When her husband got busted and sent to jail for a ten-year bid she turned to working the con game. It had been sweet for a couple of years but turned sour. My uncle, who she had met through a mutual lawyer friend, saw something special in her and asked her to give up the life and come to work for him. He said that she knew how to deal with people and that was what he needed. And that's how Honey Lavelle had come to be working in the Tease Me Club.

She told me that her marriage had produced a son, Harold. That's where Dad had come in. Her son had gotten involved with drugs. Honey needed money to send him to a rehab clinic and she didn't have it and couldn't bring herself to ask my uncle. My father advanced her the money. She paid Dad back over time and he had never mentioned it to a soul.

"I credit your father with saving my son's life," Honey said. Harold was nineteen now and going to the University of Connecticut.

"When I decide what I want to do, I'll let you know," Honey said.

"You mean to consider this a pay back or a new debt?"

"You do realize that I could consider this a new debt and demand payment right here, right now, you do understand that, Youngblood," she said smiling

"Yes, I can understand that," I smiled.

"But I don't think so."

"Why not?" I was not sure whether to feel disappointed or re-lieved.

"Because, Youngblood," she stretched her arms out and accen-tuated the line of her breasts, "when I go to gather sand from the beach, I'm not coming with a bucket, I'm coming with a dump truck," she smiled.

I laughed harder than I had in a long time. It felt good. Real good.

The sun had been doing its thing since about 8:30 in the morning. And though it was late October, the temperature had risen about ten degrees in the past twenty-four hours. Indian summer. As blocks go in New York, mine was alright, well, alright by Harlem standards anyway. The block where I live is 155th near Amsterdam Ave. and is called Sugar Hill. All of the buildings are brownstones and mostly owned by the people who live there. A brownstone is a brick building usually with four floors, large rooms, high ceilings, and wooden floors. These houses were originally built for upper class white residents who lived in Harlem prior to the black migration in the thirties and forties.

I walked down to 135th street to a brick tenement. The lobby of the tenement had the kind of beautiful architecture that had been originally designed to hold a large chandelier. It also had a fireplace that had been long since bricked up. The walls were now done up in a bright taxicab yellow, which was probably at least the twentieth coat of paint that this lobby had seen. It wasn't The Waldorf, but it was clean, the doors locked, the intercom worked, and it didn't smell of piss, which for this block in Harlem meant that the place was batting a thousand. I rode the creaking elevator to the basement. When the door opened I stepped off and was greeted by a stocky man in his mid-thirties. He wore a long beige outer garment and a matching kufi on the back of his head. He smiled at me out of a chocolate brown face framed by a neatly trimmed beard.

"As salaam alaikum," the man greeted me.

"Alaikum salaam," I responded, returning the universal Muslim greeting.

The consternation must have appeared like a mask on my face

because the man smiled and let me take a good look so that I could convince myself that my eyes were not deceiving me. When we were both sure I was seeing what I thought I was seeing, he stepped forward and hugged me.

"Didn't recognize me, huh?" he said.

"To be honest, I wasn't sure at first," I admitted.

"It's okay, don't worry, you ain't the first one who thinks they're seeing things," he laughed good-naturedly.

It was Victor Green, a man I had grown up with and had known most of my life.

"Man, you look great," I said.

"Thank you, so do you."

"You're right, I almost didn't believe it was you."

"Things can change. All praises due to Allah. Have a seat," he continued. "Pops called a minute ago to say he was running a little late, but he's on his way. He's expecting you."

Change wasn't an adequate enough word for what had happened to Victor. Metamorphosis was more like it. The last time I saw him three years ago, he was dirty, smelly, and begging in the subway high on crack. Now here he was standing in front of me, a follower of Islam and as far as I could tell a different man.

"When did you come up?"

"I'll get us some coffee," he laughed. "How do you take it?"

"Regular," I said taking a seat at one of the many small tables that bordered the shoe leather-worn wooden dance floor. In Harlem, "regular" means milk and two sugars.

Victor disappeared into the other room. Shelby had done the room up nicely. Like Uncle Beans, he also ran an after hours joint. Whereas "The Hole" is a place geared towards gamblers, Shelby's place focuses more on entertainment and dancing. At Shelby's you would find people who love music and love to dance. At the center of the huge room was a small stage set under a series of lighting grids. The lights on the metal grid affixed to the ceiling were a combination of blue, green, white, yellow, and blue spots. There was even a follow spotlight that could be shone from the back. Directly in front of the stage was a huge wooden dance floor surrounded by small tables with four chairs each. Each table was fitted with an ashtray, a vase for fresh flowers, and a candle. Back in the early sixties when Shelby first opened the club, some of the popular acts that would appear at the Apollo Theatre would find their way over to Shelby's and perform their show for cash on the side that would go straight into their pockets. Sarah Vaughn, Billy Eckstein, Marvin Gaye, The Drifters, and countless other top names had graced Shelby's stage. Now, even though the big names were not as forthcoming as in the past, the odd classic bluesman like Buckwheat James or Snake Walker and old R&B acts like the Delfonics and The Chilites still passed through from time to time. Shelby's had become a private club for the older set who were willing to pay top dollar for good old-time food, entertainment, and dancing. Shelby also ran a high stakes crap game for hustlers in the other room.

Victor returned with two cups of coffee and sat down.

I wasn't sure how to start my inquiries into his new life, so I decided to jump in with both feet.

"So when in the world did you become Muslim?" I wanted to know.

He smiled and took a sip of coffee before answering.

"I did eight months in the joint for snatching a sista's purse, and inside some Muslim brothas pulled my coat."

"Alright," I smiled, then we slapped hands the way black people often do when something has been said that demands to be punctuated in a way that mere words just won't suffice to articulate.

"What happened was funny though," Victor related. "I had been talking with the brothas inside, but I never converted, I was just interested and taking everything in, but when I got out, the state put me in this halfway house set-up where I could go to work in the daytime and come back there at night. Well I was taking the bus to work and everyday I would see this sista at the bus stop. Eventually we started kicking it a little, you know, flowing with conversation about this and that and the conversation got around to Islam. Then she invited me up to the mosque one Friday for juma prayer, you know the big one on 87th and Third. And guess what, a couple of the brothas who had been in the joint with me was there. Three weeks later I made my shahada, that was two years ago. Now I got a family and I work for my Pops. He's teaching me property management."

"That's beautiful, man," I smiled.

"Allah is Akbar, all praises due." He sipped his coffee.

The elevator opened and Shelby Green bounded into the room.

"Hey Tuffy," Shelby called across the room in my direction. "Be with you in a minute. Just getting something to drink."

Victor took his father's entrance as his cue to leave.

"Listen," he said to me, "you take care of your business with Pops and we'll hook up and rap later."

"Cool."

Victor placed his fist over his heart, winked at me, and followed his father into the other room.

Shelby returned and walked toward me with a coffee mug in hand.

Shelby had a funny, wide-legged stride that gave him the appearance of a man on a perpetual trip to the bathroom with shit in his pants. His smooth brown face, free of wrinkles, did not betray the knowledge and living he had done in his sixty-four years.

"Boy, I'll tell you, these cocksuckers got to me this morning. I been in court all motherfucking morning trying to get this deadbeat out of my place up on 145th. Today was the day the Marshall was supposed to evict him, but the Marshall was sick with the flu and the court don't want to appoint a new City Marshall, so I got to wait, which gives the deadbeat time to get another show-cause letter from the housing authority, which could set me back for another I don't know how long. It's a bitch owning property in New York, boy. Tenants can do all sorts of shit to get around paying the rent. This cocksucker ain't paid me a dime for eight months. Every month, he in court with some new shit. We need the kinds of tough laws like they got in Atlanta. In Atlanta, Georgia, guess

what, you ten days late with the rent, the landlord can get an order from the court and the Sheriff will show up on your doorstep
with a crew of men and move all your shit out of the house onto
the street. That's what we need in New York. What I would like to
do, is catch that jive deadbeat cocksucker on the street one day
and give him a good ass whipping, but the way the laws is now, I'll
wind up with a lawsuit and have to pay some more damn money.
Boy oh boy, I'll tell you Tuffy, this system is a bitch."

Shelby had called me Tuffy ever since I could remember. Dad,
Uncle Beans, Shelby Green, and Diego McMichael all had been
friends for over forty years. They had been kids in Harlem together
and had gone to the army together. They had fought for each other,
lied for each other, and laughed about it together. I knew I could
trust Shelby Green. He knew it too. At Dad's funeral, he and Uncle
Beans sat next to each other and sobbed unashamedly.

I told Shelby the whole story about Deke, Uncle Beans, the police, everything.

"Deke, that fuckin' cocksucker, never had a penny's worth of
integrity."

Shelby rarely uttered a sentence that wasn't laced with profan-
ity. He was one of the few people who could curse in front of
preachers and get away with it. Funny thing, people just always
accepted it as part of his personality. Mostly because all of his
other good qualities shone so bright that his cursing was nothing
by comparison. My grandmother used to say Shelby had a heart
made in heaven and a mouth made in hell. Shelby Green was the
kind of man who would give his last dime to help a friend and
was never too busy to do whatever he had to do to help. Besides,
being a true humanitarian, Shelby had a great head for business.
Nobody knew for sure, but by all estimates Shelby was worth at
least a couple million dollars. He never talked about it, or needed
to push his weight around, but it was no secret that Shelby owned
at least twenty buildings in Harlem. "Everybody's business ain't
nobody's business," was one of his favorite sayings.

Shelby was an old fox who knew the ins and outs of both

politics and money. When men like Uncle Beans needed to know the ramifications of real estate deals they would go to Shelby Green. Not only was he one of Harlem's most successful businessmen, he was also one of the most vocal supporters of black businesses. When the last black bank in Harlem closed down he rented a soundtruck and placed a banner on the side with the bank's name with the epitaph:

BANK OF HARLEM DEAD AND BURIED . . . GOOD.
BECAUSE YOU NEVER SUPPORTED YOUR OWN.

I explained to Shelby that the buzz on the street was that Harlem real estate agents had been selling property to Asians like it was going out of style. I also explained that two of the Asians found dead had been connected with an Asian real estate group.

"I don't know much about how the real estate game operates in Harlem, that's why I'm here."

He scratched his closed-cropped salt and pepper hair then pushed back in his seat. "Life is a funny motherfucker, Tuffy. Back in the fifties this country was kicking Korean ass by the truckload, now we kissing it by the truckload right here in Harlem. Hah."

He slammed his fist down hard on the table to emphasize the irony.

"Oh yeah," he continued, "you better believe, they buying real estate in Harlem. Buying it like ninety-nine going on a hundred."

"Any gangsters involved?"

"Damn skippy," Shelby answered. "You see these vegetable stands all over the city, they all owned by Korean gangsters. Money talks and bullshit walks don't it . . ."

He let the statement hang in the air.

"I told these niggas up here years ago when property was cheap, to buy it," he continued. "I been telling people since back in the sixties. Everybody thought I was nutty as a damn fruitcake. But didn't nobody listen except a few people like Beans and your father. Niggas was too busy buying Cadillacs, color TVs, and shit like that. Now Harlem property is prime. Where else they gonna go? Damn near everywhere else is developed in Manhattan. Columbia University done bought half of Harlem already. Wall Street people been warehousing properties for years. Now I ain't saying it's an easy thing to get money to buy property, but I tell people to do like I did, get two or three people and put your pennies together. See, not only does property generate money but it also generates political power. That's why these Koreans can come over and get power, 'cause if they don't have money they work out a deal to get it from the Korean gangsters to start their businesses. And black folks walking around Harlem madder than a motherfucker 'cause they can't get a loan to open a damn shoe shine stand, while the Korean can go in and get the money from the same bank the black folks been denied at. See, the Koreans put all of their resources together to collateralize the loan, which translates into political power, plus you don't see them driving no damn Mercedes all over the place and wearing no damn neck full of gold chains. It all comes back down to people putting their resources together. Money talks and bullshit walks."

"What does red-lining mean? I heard it talked about but I don't really understand it," I said.

"Red-lining is when the bank makes a decision that a certain area is unprofitable to make loans to. They usually do it on the basis of income of residents and the likelihood of a business succeeding in certain communities but the reality is, more often than not, it's done based on the race of the people living in the neighborhood."

"Red-lining is illegal, right?"

"So is prostitution and the selling of drugs," Shelby shrugged. "So what else is new. Most things that make money are illegal somewhere down the line but, you know as well as I do, the minute somebody sits down to come up with a new law, the big boys making money at that game sit down on the other side of the same table and start to come up with a way to circumvent that new law that's going to affect their money making. That's just the way the motherfucking big money game is played. Forget about who's right or wrong, everybody just accepts it as part of how business is done. That's America, baby. Money talks and bullshit walks. I'm gon tell you something, I'm gon tell you something crazy . . ."

I sat back. Shelby was on a roll.

"You know Doc Johnson?"

"Doc Johnson?" I frowned.

"Sure you do, Tuffy, old Doc Johnson, the dentist had the office on 140th. Big red man, always wore light suits and drove a white Rolls."

"Oh yeah," I said as the memory flashed in my brain.

"You know, Doc passed away about six months ago, and left his building to his son Willis."

"Yeah, I know his son."

"Well, Willis is an only child, and is as dumb as a fucking box of rocks. A Japanese man comes to my office looking for a property. So I put him on to Willis, 'cause Willis don't really know nothing about property, he was just living there mismanaging it and letting the property go all to hell. I figured, I'd help him sell it, make a nice broker's fee and Willis could put a few dollars in the bank, you know. So I set up the deal. I talk to Willis and to the Jap and we agree on a price — $215,000 cash. So the man offers to take Willis to a nice Japanese restaurant to seal the deal. Willis is all excited and grateful and shit. Everything is everything. The man, me, and Willis all agree to meet at the restaurant. I'm supposed to bring the papers, we're going to have dinner, sign the papers, and the man will give Willis a cashier's check on the following day. Everything is everything, right. I prepare the papers. In the agreement I put the clause in that if the money is not forthcoming on the following day, the deal is null and void. Okay, everybody is covered, everything is set. Anyway, Willis shows up at the restaurant with this broad. This crazy ass Brazilian HooDoo broad."

"HooDoo?" I echoed.

"Yeah, HooDoo. You know, the kind of broad who fucks with spirits and shit, casting spells and shit. First thing the waiter in the restaurant asks is that we take off our shoes. We take off our shoes and sit down cross-legged and the man asks what we want to eat then he orders in Japanese for us. Well the food comes and the broad starts acting like a jackass. She go to smelling the damn food and talking about the food is giving off weird spirit energy. So she starts chanting some weird blessing all over the food in a loud ass voice. Now the Japanese man ain't used to no crazy niggas like this broad, so he starts getting nervous and confused. Me, I'm trying to cool everything out 'cause I got the deal all set up and, next thing you know, the waiter bring in this hot green colored Japanese horse radish mustard called *wasabe* and Willis with his pig ass bitch start to smear this shit all over their meat. Then the Japanese man tells Willis that he don't want to eat too much of this stuff on his meat 'cause this shit is hot sho nuff. Then the broad jumps up and says the Japanese hot stuff wasn't nothing compared to what they got back in Brazil, so she reaches over into Willis' plate and gulps down two pieces of meat. Next thing you know all hell breaks loose. 'Cause the shit is so strong that it takes her damn breath away and she can't catch her damn breath back. Willis think that the man done tried to poison his woman, so Willis reaches over across the table and slaps the Japanese man in the face. Then the crazy HooDoo bitch jumps up on the table with her big ugly nasty ass looking feet. Feet so nasty it turned my stomach. She knocked all the damn food all over the floor and she started to chanting and whooping and hollering and rolling all over the floor like some wild ass Indian. Everybody in the restaurant looking at us now like we stark raving mad. And the Japanese man's nose is bleeding from where Willis slapped him. Damn. Man, I never been so damned embarrassed in my whole life."

The laughter kept building up inside me the more I listened to Shelby. He could have been a comedian with the talent he had for telling a funny story.

"Anyway, by now the Japanese man wants to pull out altogether.

He just wants to get away from this crazy bitch and her fool ass man, and I don't blame him. So I go home with him and tell him not to worry I would deliver the papers and everything could be done through me. So now I go over to talk to this fool ass Willis but this HooDoo broad keep telling him that the Japanese man tried to poison her, and this fool is now saying that the deal is off. Then she says that the man ain't serious 'cause he didn't bring his money with him. So I try to explain to this asshole, that folks don't walk around with $215,000 in chump change, but she don't want to hear it and she got him so worked up that he don't want to hear anything either. They both decide all they want is cash. I keep trying to explain that I'll bring the money in the morning, but Willis is totally under the influence of this crazy ass broad, so now he keeps saying that he don't trust the man to have the money. Says he want cash on the barrel head. What a goddamn fool, huh? So then I get a bright idea, see," Shelby continued. "I go home and manage to make a few quick calls and I come up with about forty thousand cash. I put it into two suitcases and I get Victor to go with me back over to see Willis. See, I know this broad is crazy but I can see she ain't no fool. She wants to be in control and she's money hungry — otherwise why would she be going around with Willis. But she too stupid to see how things is moving. Like I said, I can see she crazy but she ain't no fool, and I was right too, 'cause when I dumped them two suitcases full of money onto the bed, the bitch damn near had a stroke. After she saw that money I did not hear one more word of that chanting shit. Her eyes damn near popped out of her head. Man, she grabbed that ink pen from me and put it into that fool Willis' hand and told him to sign the paper, and just like a child with no questions asked he signed the paper. Next day I had the property transferred to my name and then went and collected $215,000 from the Japanese man, paid Willis, and took my commission. Now, you tell me, you ever hear of anything so crazy in your damn life?"

"Incredible," I said through the tears that had formed in my eyes from laughter.

Shelby took it further. "They took the money and guess what these fools did? They rented a swanky place down in the village for five grand a month. Can you believe that? Shit, Rockefeller don't even pay that kinda rent. Then they spent over ten thousand making this broad a record album. Willis talking about he revitalizing her singing career. What career, bitch was selling chew sticks and perfume in a booth at the African market up on 116th when he met her, what goddamn singing career? And I ain't saying I know nothing technically about music, but I know one thing, the money Willis spent on that record was just money thrown into the garbage can. 'Cause I swear if that crazy broad can sing then my dick can sing. That fool ass Willis talking about, he gon' get her record on the radio. When I fart I sound better than she do singing. I'll tell you boy, the fools they got in Harlem. But that ain't the worse part. Oh you ain't heard the worst yet. With the biggest part of the money they opened up a tanning salon in Harlem. Of all the places in the world with all the fucking black folks in the world, they open up a goddamn tanning salon. And don't you know they were broke in four months. Must have got ten customers in four months. And after all of Willis's money was gone, the crazy broad left him. Fool ass fool negro didn't even have a place to stay. I felt sorry for him, so I gave him an apartment in exchange for some janitorial work he supposed to be doing for me. But boy, I'll tell you, I ain't never seen anything like it in my life. That took the cake. Have you ever heard of anything so goddamn crazy in your life? Shit. But to answer your question about there being Asians buying up property in Harlem for cash, the answer is yes, definitely yes."

Sunday, 4:30 P.M.
■ A Rented Room Somewhere in Harlem

*T*he angel extracted the needle from the brown bottle and inserted it into the man's vein. His body shivered as the drug caught hold and surged into his bloodstream providing the rush that brought the screaming inside his head to a halt. It was always the drug that cleared the messy mass of contortions taking place inside his head, and sent the monster of confusion back into its dark cave. The morphine galloped inside his veins like a racing thoroughbred and altered his conscious state of being. The angel reached down and kissed the man with the dead eyes. She touched and kissed him in places no woman had ever touched and kissed him before. Then she put her mouth close to his ear. The vibration from her voice washed over, warmed, calmed, and satisfied him, almost as much as the morphine did. In some ways even more. The morphine was only sustenance, but his angel was pure energy, the ultimate life force radiating in the form of flesh and blood. She was his angel. And he was her man with the dead eyes.

"We are close, so close," she purred into his ear. "That's why we must not stop. We must finish what we started. I want you to make this thing work for me. Do it for me if you love me," she said.

Her honey-colored skin wrapped around his hard ugly body as she guided him into the act of physical lovemaking. The angel was an expert at making him find feelings that he didn't know existed.

"They have your picture. That's why you must do it now. I promise I will do my part, but you also must promise me that you will do your part, okay?" she said as she moved up and down rhythmically on top of him. Her nakedness caressed him, soothing the pain inside his being. It took away the years of loneliness, almost even made up for the time his mother left him at Big Sam's and never came back.

"Okay," was all he said.

The angel smiled, because she knew that an okay from the man with the dead eyes was enough. She turned her mind away from what her body was doing. She thought about the Mediterranean sun and walking barefoot in the South of France. She thought about ice skating on Lake Placid in upstate New York. She thought about dancing naked on the white sands of Jamaica in the moonlight. She thought about Carnival in Rio. She thought about an Asian cooking class she wanted to take. She thought about an old friend from her college days who she wanted to visit in Europe. She thought about a new sports car she planned to buy. The angel thought about many things, but not one had anything to do with what her body was doing at the moment.

After they finished making love, the angel washed the body of the man with the dead eyes. Then she fed him hot beef stew that she had bought at a take-out restaurant down the block. As he ate it she kissed him. The man with the dead eyes was content and in love with his angel. His angel understood the magic and the power of love. She understood that a man's love could be more powerful than an entire army.

After the man with the dead eyes had fallen asleep, the angel left.

Sunday, 8:30 P.M.
■ Be-Bop Tavern

The poster sketch of the murder suspect was now all over Harlem, and the calls came in by the hundreds. The cover story we made up for the media was that the man in the sketch was wanted in connection with the mugging of an old lady who was still in the hospital. A reward of $500 was being offered for information leading to his arrest. The poster told people that the man was dangerous and was not to be approached, but simply to report his whereabouts to the police. Scheming sisters called in the names of hated brothers, dissatisfied wives called in the names of unfaithful husbands, gilded girlfriends called in the names of former boyfriends. A broken-hearted transvestite even called in the name of his former lover who was also a transvestite. It seemed that anybody who had a grudge against anybody called in to report them and claim the reward.

A lot of leads had been followed up, but nobody had been charged. Mack and I were hopeful that someone would eventually call in with the right information. We were tired. I checked with a ticket hustler who was a regular on tickets for the Knicks and was able to get two seats on the floor of Madison Square Garden for Onion. They cost me a pretty penny, but I got them anyway. Money came and went but there was only one Onion.

Mack and I kept beating our heads against the wall for a new angle, hoping for another break. Trying to I.D. some clue or link that we had missed, but we couldn't think of anything. Mack suggested that we get a list of all the people involved with my uncle on the Landmark Committee on the theory that if Sun Bright contacted Lee then they may have contacted someone else. Someone else, especially some other Asian who might be in danger. To be honest, I didn't have much hope that this line would get us very far. Mack admitted that he didn't either really, but we both admitted it was better than doing nothing. We had come to a standstill. The pieces were there, but they wouldn't fit together. I called Uncle Beans at the office and he told me that Miss Pritchard would fax a list of the Landmark Committee membership over to me. He asked me to call him later at Barbara's house, then Miss Pritchard came on the line. She promised to send the fax ASAP, then quite abruptly changed the subject.

"To be honest Marcus, I needed to speak to you anyway. I am very worried about your Uncle's stomach," she said. "He naturally has a nervous stomach and I know what he can and can't eat. I should know, I've been cooking for him for almost twenty years. And Mrs. Simmons is not as aware of that. Honestly, I think it could be her fancy food that's causing his discomfort. I spoke to Kit and we both agreed that the only one he really listens to is you."

I told her I would try and convince him to listen to her advice. On top of everything else I was being pushed into the middle of a domestic squabble by Miss Pritchard who was no doubt reacting to being replaced by Barbara as the most influential woman in Uncle Beans' life. I was feeling like the words from the old blues song: "Some days it just don't pay to even get out of bed."

The fax came and I looked through the list of Landmark Committee members. There were five names listed as voting members — the deceased Mr. Lee, Uncle Beans, Mr. Morris, Attorney Philip Jackson, and Mrs. Lambrusky. Barbara Simmons and Tony Wilborne were listed as non-voting members.

It was 10:00 P.M. and the bar was still buzzing in full swing. Les McCann singing "Compared To What" blared from the jukebox, as the weekend partygoers did their weekend things. I was wiping down the bar when I looked up and saw Deke Robinson standing at the window grinning from ear to ear.

"I just want to congratulate you on the fine job," Deke said. "Can I buy you a drink?"

"Naw, working," was my lame excuse.

"Rum and water," Deke said.

I poured the drink and took his money.

"Sure you won't join me?" Deke offered again.

"No, I'm cool."

He pushed out his hand for me to shake and smiled. I accommodated him.

"Varney told me that you guys found the girl that saw the killings, so as far as downtown is concerned the heat's not on so hot. At least we've given the Republicans a dummy target to point the finger at for the time being. It buys time for the boys downtown, which is a good thing all around.

"I guess the drug dealers can sleep peacefully again, huh?" I said sarcastically.

I could see the anger starting to boil up in Deke's face. I had upset him and insulted his fake pride.

"Listen, Devil, why don't you stop acting so holier than thou, you got dirt on your hands just like the rest of us. CIA dirt. How many people did you take out? How many innocent people did you kill?"

"I did my share," I admitted. "But that was then."

"Oh so you suddenly get religion, and the world becomes a terrible place, huh?"

"No, not that at all. What I did, I did. No excuses. My problem with you is that you know you're helping to fuck up black peoples lives and you still tiptoe through the tulips without giving it a second thought. But who am I to judge Deke, I'm just a neighborhood bartender," I said with a smirk.

"Yeah, who are you to judge?" he echoed.

"I ain't judging nobody, but maybe if Harlem didn't have a Deke Robinson running around buying votes and giving protection to the drug dealers, maybe my Dad would be alive today, that's how I think about it, Deke," I said wiping down the bar and looking him dead in the eye.

"You damn hypocrite. What do you think your uncle is doing with those clubs he owns, with all the gambling joints? You don't see that as taking money out of black peoples pockets and fucking up black peoples lives. He don't care who he gets it from as long as the money is green."

"Maybe, but at least he lives here and puts something back once in a while. What have you given back, Deke?"

He laughed. "Bullshit, compare what he gives back with the money he makes off of election fixing, his rake off on gambling and shady real estate deals and you can bet what he puts back is just a pittance."

"Just like the rest of us, he's got to pay for his own sins."

"Remember Devil, you might have grown up here, but you're still the new kid on the block. You've been away for a long time . . ."

"You have too, Deke," I reminded him.

"But I've been back long enough to find out where some pretty heavy bones are buried. I suggest you cool out until you've been around a while. I'm much more valuable as a friend than as an enemy."

"I don't think so."

"Have it your way, sport."

With that Deke turned and walked out.

As I watched him go I realized that one day I might have to put an end to Deke Robinson's political career, possibly even his life. A fact which didn't bother me in the least. Actually I was kind of looking forward to the occasion.

Mack met me at 11:00 P.M. I showed him the Landmark Committee list.

"Who controls the 'at large' seats?" he asked.

"My uncle controls both of them but they are non-voting," I explained. "Lee voted with my uncle. They had mutual tax interests. Attorney Jackson and Mrs. Lambrusky wanted to sell out to Sun Bright Realty rather than develop the Landmark properties as tax shelters and Morris is said to be leaning towards voting my uncles' way."

"I see," Mack said. "We have the information but it doesn't mean much. Like a rowboat in the water without oars."

We agreed that tomorrow we would begin to make contact with the Landmark Committee members. I checked on Peter Pan and she was doing okay. Her schedule for the day was eating and watching music videos on TV. Mack left and said he'd be back in a hour. He departed bouncing happily and whistling the theme tune from the play, *The Little Shop of Horrors.*

I poured a lot of drinks, listened to a few tales of woe from my customers, played a few selections on the jukebox, then sent out for Indian food and watched basketball — Miami and Houston on cable. I called Kit but she was out. I left a message on her machine and forty-five minutes later she called back.

"Hey babygirl, just checking in, how's tricks?"

"Good, Larry just invited me to the Bahamas to celebrate my passing the bar," she told me. I could hear the grin in her voice.

"What it look like then?" I teased.

"All it look like is that I'm going to be getting some sunshine and that's all," she said coyly, "What's up with you?"

"I talked to Miss Pritchard earlier, who said that Barbara don't know how to cook for one thing," I laughed.

"Hey, that's just the way Miss Pritchard is, honey. Barbara is messing with her precious Mr. Johnson, so I guess that's just her way of peeing on a tree and marking off her territory," Kit laughed.

"I guess so," I said joining her in the joke.

"Daddy told me this morning that his stomach has been feeling a little better At least, he wasn't complaining this morning. From all I can see Barbara has been taking care of him okay. She should be able to, she used to be a nurse. Listen," she said changing the subject, "do me a favor and please get your one modern suit cleaned and pressed because next week I've got somebody coming into town I want you to meet."

"One of your goon crew buddies, why do I have to wear my one modern suit?" I complained lightheartedly.

"Goon crew nothing, this girl is the bomb, and I don't want you looking like you just walked off the set of *Men In Black* with those plain dull colors you be wearing. Hook up nice, it will be well worth it, you'll like Brenda, trust me."

"Like the time I trusted you to make Kool-Aid for my high school graduation party and you put salt in it, instead of sugar. Oh yeah, I trust you alright."

She laughed recalling the memory.

"Gotta run, see you later."

"See ya," I said and hung up smiling.

It was almost 11:00 and Christine had things well under control. I decided to take it easy until about twelve o'clock then I would go home. I needed the rest. To my surprise I looked up and saw Al Mack standing on the other side of the bar grinning directly at me like a cheshire cat. Mack was all decked out in a brown sports jacket and a black shirt opened at the collar rather than in the dark gray business suit that he usually wore.

"Man," Mack began, "I got to thinking. We been busting our humps all week on this thing, right. What I figured we both could use is a little R&R, you know, take our minds off of this thing. What made me think about it was these," he said holding up two tickets on which I could see the words *Blue Note* printed in bright blue letters. I know how much you dig jazz, so I got my sister-in-law who works in Ticketron to do me a solid. These are two tickets to a one time only midnight performance with Marlene Campbell tonight. Interested?"

There was only one Marlene Campbell, I didn't even have to think twice. My body needed rest, but my soul needed her more.

"Just let me stop by the crib to change my clothes and shower. It'll take fifteen minutes," I grinned back looking at my watch. I knew we could drive down the Westside Highway and make it to the Village in twenty minutes, park in the garage across from the Blue Note, and be inside with five minutes to spare.

Ten minutes later I pulled up in front of my place. Mack followed in the sedan. He found a parking place in front of the house, while I parked in my usual spot on the same block further down the street.

"This is a nice crib. You grow up here?" Mack asked as he looked up at the building and we started up the steps.

"Yeah, all my life."

I inserted my key into the lock and with my peripheral vision saw the blurring movement behind me. I turned to see a flash of steel ramming into Mack under his armpit. Mack lurched forward causing me to slam into the door. I mule kicked backward catching the assailant squarely in the groin. I heard him grunt and watched him fall backwards down three steps as I spun around. The impact of the kick caused the attacker to release the knife from his right hand.

The knife fell to the last step, then onto the sidewalk. The weapon flashed in my mind. Bowie knife, ten-inch blade, commando issue. The man recovered the knife. I dropped my upper body to the ground in a spinning cartwheeling motion and kicked him again, this time in the face. The blow sent him reeling backwards causing his head to hit the top of Mack's sedan. I recognized him as the man in the police sketch. The knife went sailing over the car top into the street. He was dazed and I was ready to move in and make the kill when I heard Mack moan. One kick to the base of my attacker's skull would have severed his spinal chord. The moment was now. Mack moaned again louder, distracting me for that one precious second, and the man scampered out of kicking range and disappeared into the darkness like a fleeing ghost

Mack lay slumped over on my doorstep moaning and gasping for air. I could see where the knife had entered and, from the way he was breathing, I knew the steel blade had punctured his lung. I sat him upright and began screaming at the top of my voice for help. Mr. Humphrey from next door came to his door dressed in a bathrobe and wearing a stocking cap on his head.

"Call 911, tell them a policeman has been stabbed, tell them to hurry!"

Mr. Humprey nodded and disappeared back into the house.

Mack moaned again, louder this time.

"Hold on, baby, just hold on It ain't as bad as it feels, just hold on," I said hoping he wouldn't pass out. His eyes had glazed over and he continued to swallow and gasp for air. His lungs were filling up with fluid. I watched helplessly as Mack lay helpless, slowly drowning in his own blood.

The ambulance arrived within minutes. The crew began their work and I moved out of the way. With the help of somebody's flashlight, I found the knife where it had landed.

I used a piece of cardboard from an abandoned cereal box to pick it up, then got a clean plastic bag from Mr. Humprey and dropped the blade inside. The neighborhood folk had gathered around the ambulance to see what there was to see. The whole incident had taken place in less than fifteen minutes. I felt myself growing cold inside as I watched Mack with his face under the oxygen mask being carted off by the ambulance with its sirens screaming into the murky October night.

I arrived at the hospital five minutes behind the ambulance. Mack was already in the operating room. Three hours later, I was still there waiting to find out if he would make it or not. I must have dozed off because the next thing I remember was a smallish white woman with red hair addressing me.

"I'm Doctor O'Mally," she said with a slight Irish accent.

"Is he still alive?" I said sitting up and preparing to hear the worst. Old habits are hard to break especially when you have heard the final report as many times as I had.

"Yes, we've done all that we can for now. From this point on we'll just have to wait. He's just being transferred to intensive care."

"What are his chances?"

"Only God knows that. I've seen them better and worse. A lot will depend on his will to stay alive."

I didn't answer. A feeling of immense caring for Al Mack seemed to rise up in my chest blocking my voice.

"You don't look too good yourself, better go get some rest, there's nothing you can do here," the doctor told me.

In a way I wanted to thank her, but in another way I wanted to give her a piece of my mind. I wanted to tell her that Al Mack was more than just another statistic, that he was a husband and a father and how much he would be missed if he died. But I didn't. I took her advice and headed home to rest. The only thing I could do now was to pray. I just hoped God was listening.

Back in my apartment, I tried to push the thought of Al Mack away from the front of my mind. I went to the kitchen and drank what was left from an opened carton of orange juice and ate half a can of tuna that I had left over from the day before. I flopped down on the couch and put on an Ella Fitzgerald CD. By now the rain had begun to tap a syncopated rhythm on my window as Ella sang from the Gershwin songbook. Just as I began to doze the phone rang. It was Honey's voice, that much I remembered. But I was all wrapped up in a world of sleep. I mumbled something that must have been, "Yeah, okay," then slipped deeply back into the heart of dreamland.

I don't recall any of the details but I do recall the colors, all soft blues and browns floating around like the notes in a Lester Young saxophone solo. I was feeling it and the funny thing was, I still smelled the rain. The beautiful soft dream was washing the world's confusion off into the abyss of oblivion when suddenly the phone screamed again and all of my soft hues turned a puke-colored green.

I awoke with a cloud of confusion covering my brain like a veil.

It was Christine's voice pitched in a worried tone.

"Yeah."

"Something weird is happening here."

I fought to clear the fog inside my head.

"Weird?"

"Yeah. You okay, you sound funny?"

"Just waking up," I managed, with my tongue still thick in my mouth. "What's happening?"

"A man has been standing around outside the bar. He didn't come in. He just keeps coming by, looking in the window again and again."

"What man, can you describe him?"

"A black man, well I think it's a black man. It's hard to tell."

"He might be just a wino or something," I said, not wanting to panic her.

"I just thought I'd better tell you," she said.

"You did right. Where's Duke?"

"He finished cleaning up and left about a half hour ago, after the last customer. You still locking up, right?"

"Me? Ok, yeah." Shit! I had forgotten. Tonight was my night to lock up. "Okay, just make sure the front door is locked and I'll be right down. On my way."

I hung up and picked up my .38 from under my mattress and

jammed it into the waistband of my pants, pulled on a wind-breaker, and raced three at a time down the stairs. Outside, it was raining cats and dogs. I should have worn my rain gear, but it was too late now. My car was parked on the next block. I ran the distance, jumped in and started to drive.

Ten minutes later, I pulled up in front of the Be-Bop. The block was deserted except for the rain, and a crackhead hooker standing in a nearby doorway. She had just scored and was beaming up between tricks.

The lights were still on inside the bar. Christine was nowhere in sight. I eased the revolver from my waistband then walked slowly from the car to the entrance of the bar. As I unlocked the front door, Christine appeared from the back.

"Anything since we spoke?" I inquired, backing inside with an eye out for any sudden move from the shadows.

"No, I haven't seen him again. I'm sorry I just got a little nervous."

"No, you did exactly right. Better safe than sorry." I shivered.

"You'd better get into some dry things," Christine said.

"Yeah."

I changed into a set of work clothes that I kept on hand. As I changed I thought about the possibilities. It could be the man who attacked Al out there. If the guy was still lurking around, he would have seen me come in and would be waiting.

I called a cab for Christine. One friend was already lying in the hospital, I didn't want it to happen again.

The cab pulled up a few moments later and Christine jumped in and rode off. I turned off the lights in the Be-Bop and stepped back into the street. The rain had not let up, not even an inch. With my pistol still in hand, I made my way slowly and cautiously back to the car. There were no sudden movements from the shadows. Now only the pouring rain and a lonely dismal mood inhabited the streets. As I headed home I realized I was soaked again. I turned the fan heater on high. It helped a little but not much. To make it worse my insides were turning to ice and sharp pains were moving from deep in the middle of my back up into my neck. Danger. *Danger.* My mind was playing the same message over and over. Got to get home. Got to get home into the bed with the heating pads. You'll be alright. Just get home to your warm bed. When I reached my block if was almost 4:38 A.M. My mind was dull and my body was screaming to me through the growing pain. Rest. Relax. Rest. Relax. *Danger zone!* The closest that I could park to my building was half a block away. I hated the thought of getting soaked again but there was no choice. I knew that after I got a hot shower, drank lots of water, and placed my body against a couple of heating pads the pain might subside.

I jumped from the car and out the corner of my eye, I saw a Jeep pull from the curb and head in my direction. Instinct drove my body and I pivoted to the right. The Jeep sped past missing me by a few inches. I went crashing into a row of garbage cans. My revolver slipped from my hands and skidded across the pavement just out of reach. A fat, greasy rat darted from an overturned can and sprinted across my leg in a mad dash back to safety. I used my left hand to regain my balance as I positioned my legs under me and pushed myself up. A fire rose like lava in a volcano inside my ankles and exploded in my knees.

Somehow I managed to struggle up and find my feet to see that the Jeep had crashed into the stoop. The door of the Jeep swung open and a man stumbled out. It was raining too hard and he was wearing a hood plus his face was all covered in blood. I couldn't see who he was. His legs gave way and he crumbled down to the pavement, but I was too sick and weak to go over and kick the shit out of him. A jolt of pain traveled down my body almost taking my breath away. Somehow I made it to my front steps. I pulled myself up the steps slowly. Each step was like moving my knees through a red-hot fire. I wanted to live. Needed to live. I felt my body pass through the door of my living room as the blackness of pain closed in, extinguishing my consciousness with each new step. Fuck, I could hear heavy footsteps coming up behind me. My gun, I needed my gun . . .

I collapsed onto the floor. The footsteps came closer. Inside my mind, I feared I was a dead man. The darkness of the unconscious closed in further as an atomic bomb exploded inside my body. Pain burned like a three-alarm fire as it traveled through my veins. Then . . . Footsteps. Desperately clinging to the concept of life and still in total agony, I lost consciousness.

My mind was a violent tornado, blowing and tossing my thoughts and emotions against the jagged surfaces of my psyche. Blood spurted up and splattered into my eyes, blocking out my vision. I saw Satan beckoning and laughing.

Time passed and eventually the tornado lessened. The storm died and there was suddenly a calm blue sea. The blue water then turned a deep purple and the sky turned from a dark, dismal, and dirty green to a lighter milky gray mixed with the yellow of the sun that began to shine through. I opened my eyes. Honey Lavelle was sitting there mopping my forehead with a damp cloth. My bones ached but I felt warm. The point of the spear being jabbed into my nerve endings had been dulled. I recognized the feeling. It was a narcotic drowsiness. Honey was smiling down at me and I was laying in my bed.

"Am I still alive?"

"Yes, you are very much alive Youngblood. You passed out. You had a sickle cell crisis. I called Mrs. Pritchard and she told me what to do."

The flashback of the car trying to run me over came back vividly.

"Someone tried to kill me." My throat was very dry. "Tried to run me over."

"I know," Honey said sympathetically.

"You know?"

"I was sitting in my car, I saw it," she said.

"The man, did you see him?"

"Yes, but not clearly, it was raining hard. But he was hurt though. I saw him limp off when people started coming outside to see what had happened."

"How did you come to be there?"

"Don't you remember, I called you earlier and I told you I was coming by tonight."

I thought back, but I couldn't remember. Oh yeah, I did remember Honey's voice on the phone, but not what she had said to me.

"I think maybe you need to get to the hospital," she said.

"No, I'll be alright, I just need to rest."

Then it suddenly dawned on me that I was in my own pajamas.

"Who changed my clothes?"

"I did, why are you embarrassed?" She smiled.

"No, just grateful, thank you."

She lifted up a cup of warm tea to my lips and placed a pill in my mouth. I didn't want it, but I was still too weak to protest. I knew the taste, it was dyhydracodiene.

"This is your second one, I gave you one before," Honey explained.

"How long have I been out?"

"About forty minutes."

"I'll take this one but no more," I said and swallowed the pill.

"You left your front door wide open, so I followed you up the stairs when you came in," Honey continued. "But we can talk about that later, right now you need to rest."

Honey adjusted the heating pad and kissed me on the forehead. She then clicked off the light and walked into the living room. The clock by my bed read 5:50 A.M.

Almost. He had almost gotten me. Two attempts in one night. I didn't feel scared or shaken. My CIA training had long since gotten me past those emotional boundaries. Now it was just a matter of thinking to the next time. Twice he had tried and twice he had failed. The next time one of us would surely die. As for me, I strangely remembered that the week before I had ordered my tickets to a big band concert celebrating the works of Duke Ellington and Count Basie, which was taking place in only five days. This was a concert I wasn't hardly planning to miss.

The smell of hospitals all over the world is the same. They have that antiseptic stench that travels through your nose and gets into your body, creating a queasiness in the stomach. Why do all these places that are supposed to make people well smell so sickening? I read through my eighth magazine and looked at my watch again. Mack had been in intensive care all night and day and was still on the critical list.

I hated hospitals. In a way I'm glad Dad had died quickly, because Mom had not. In her final days, they let me visit her. She had grown weak and thin with a faraway look in her watery eyes. It was like she was somebody who used to be my Mom. My real Mom had left that body a long time ago. I had that same feeling as I stood and watched Amanda. Ironically, I had watched Amanda die while she was still connected to a life support machine.

The operation had gone wrong. The front office had called it an administrative oversight. The Agency had gotten word that the Mexican government was on the lookout for illegals coming into the U.S. who traded sensitive documents for passage. The documents involved classified information about oil deposits, and other sensitive stuff. Our job had been to infiltrate the information smugglers' operation. Julio was one of the smugglers involved. Amanda was his sister. She was into smuggling people not classified information. The people she dealt with were all poor and looked to the States for a better way of life.

To make a long story short, we met and fell in love.

Neither one of us expected it. It just happened. It lasted for five months until the CIA decided to stage a raid on Julio's operation without my knowledge.

Fifteen people died including Julio. Amanda was critically

wounded. She was shipped out to the hospital and put on a life support machine. I watched her for days on end until one by one her vital organs stopped functioning on their own. Her relatives eventually told the doctors to disconnect the machine. Amanda died never knowing my true identity.

I hated hospitals.

It was almost 4:30 P.M. when the doctor came to inform Mack's family that his condition had not improved one way or the other and that he was still in a coma.

"Do you think he'll make it?" his wife Elizabeth turned to me and asked in desperation. She was short and brown with plump round features. She held a Bible in her hand.

"Honestly, I don't know, we'll just have to wait and see." I hugged her and she hugged me back.

"Al said you were a real special guy, just like your father," Elizabeth said.

Emotion rose once again in my chest blocking my speech.

Elizabeth simply nodded her head and walked away. She didn't confer with any of the relatives who had accompanied her. She just walked back and sat in the corner she had occupied for the whole time and quietly resumed praying for her husband of seventeen years.

I stayed until the evening, around 6:00 P.M., hoping and waiting for some change in Mack's condition, but nothing changed so I left. Throughout the day my mind was divided. Half was with Mack at the hospital, the other half with the man who had put him there.

I called Onion and gave him all seven names on the Landmark Committee list.

"You are a busy man these days, I see," Onion said.

"I am unfortunately, but yes."

"Is tomorrow soon enough?" he wanted to know.

"I'd prefer today, if possible," I coaxed. "By the way those Knicks tickets, I couldn't get the whole series. But I did getcha two of the games in the five-game series against the Bulls."

"You got 'em?" Onion's voiced raised an octave with excitement. "Hey Jess," he called to his wife, "Dev got us tickets to the Knicks and the Bulls, two nights, can you believe it?"

In the background I could hear Jesse picking up the cheering and shouting with joy.

"Thanks, how much do I owe you?" asked Onion

"You owe me uh," I paused purposely keeping him in suspense. "Nothing, it's on the house."

"Wow," Onion said appreciatively with the enthusiasm of a child. "Thanks, Dev."

"Talk to you later."

Fatigue hit me again like a ton of bricks. I went home, careful when I entered that no one was waiting for me either on the front steps or on the landing. Inside, I took the 9mm Baretta from the china cabinet and checked the house throughout to make sure I was alone. I checked my answering machine. Honey had called. I returned her call.

"What are you doing now?" Honey asked, her voice full of genuine concern.

"About to catch a nod, I'm beat."

"Be careful, I'll call you later."

"Okay."

"You planning to go back to the hospital tonight?" she asked.

"Yeah, why?"

"Maybe I'll meet you there, and afterwards, we can stop back by my place. You like greens?"

"Yeah, that sounds good. Okay, call you when I wake up."

I made a sandwich from some leftover roast beef that I'd bought earlier in the week and ate a cold slice of sweet potato pie. I called my uncle to fill him in. I left a message on his machine, then I tried Barbara's. He wasn't there either so I left another message, on her machine this time. Just in case, I left Honey's number for him to reach me. I clicked on the TV hoping to catch some of the basketball game, but all I caught was the back of my eyelids.

It was 8:55 P.M. when I woke up. I showered, changed clothes,

and called Honey. A half hour later we met in intensive care.
Mack's wife Elizabeth, I was told, had gone home an hour ago.
The duty nurse allowed us to go into the room where Mack was
being monitored. She made me turn off my cell phone and
beeper while I was inside, which I did. All of the tubes, monitors,
IV bags, and charts that accompanied such cases were present
and accounted for. Mack's skin seemed a pale shade of gray and
he looked a lot smaller lying down with the sheets pulled up
to his chest. There was a tube down his throat helping him to
breath. That tube was connected to a life-sustaining respirator. I
fought my mind to keep from thinking about Amanda. But I did
anyway.

"I'm sorry, really sorry," Honey said. "Mack's a nice guy."

"Yeah," I smiled.

"Let's walk," Honey said.

We went into the lobby area and sat. We talked about life.
Talked about life in a room where death hung like a rain cloud in
a darkening sky. I thought about my cell phone and switched it
back on. I smiled, looked at Honey then looked away again.

"What's wrong?" she asked.

"I was trying to imagine you as a singer."

"Oh you were, were you. I wasn't bad in my day," she grinned.

"What kind of music did you sing?"

"Mostly jazz. Sarah Vaughn, Ella Fitzgerald, torch songs mostly."
I was impressed.

"Really, you can sing Ella's songs?"

"Yeah, I told you I was a singer. I studied, you know."

"Classical?"

"And jazz," she smiled sweetly.

"I just never thought of you as a jazz singer, I'd thought maybe
R&B, funky stuff, you know."

"You've asked me twenty questions, there is something I would
like to ask you."

"Shoot."

"How did you get the name Devil?"

"It started out as Little Devil, it was a nickname my grand-mother started calling me because she said sometimes when I was in my highchair I would refuse all food if I didn't have who I wanted feeding me. After I got older the little part was dropped.

"If you started acting up that early, you must really be a pistol now," she laughed.

When Honey smiled, I noticed how her face crinkled into tiny crow's feet at the corner of her eyes. Not the kind that made a woman look old, but the kind that made her look experienced and sophisticated. Sexy.

Moments like these were dangerous. The fragility of life made people sensitive. And sensitivity made people vulnerable and vulnerability made people think thoughts like I was thinking. Like how much I really liked Honey and hoped that maybe she really liked me too. I realized that now was not the time and place to think such thoughts, but I found myself thinking them anyway. My cell phone rang. On the other end was Miss Pritchard's voice.

"Marcus, this is Mamie Pritchard." Her voice was strained. An alarm went through my body. Because in all the years I had known her, she was never fussed. Always cool.

"Yes."

"Your uncle is with me now. We are on our way to Harlem Hospital. He was delivering me some papers and he just doubled over with pain. I'm taking him there now. Where are you?"

"I'm already at the hospital, a friend of mine got stabbed last night."

"Oh my," Miss Pritchard said. "Well you stay right there I'm bringing him in now to emergency."

I could hear my uncle's voice protesting in the background, but he was out-gunned.

"Stay there, okay?" she repeated and hung up.

I explained the call to Honey who said exactly what I was thinking.

"When it rains it pours."

In fifteen minutes my uncle had arrived. He was walking, slightly bent over but otherwise he looked okay.

"How are you feeling?" Honey asked him first.

"I'm fine. Mamie's just driving me crazy, that's all."

Miss Pritchard was being her normal, efficient self, marshaling the hospital staff to check Uncle Beans out immediately. We waited another hour until the doctor had started running tests on him.

I told Miss Pritchard to call me as soon as she found out the status of the tests. She promised she would. Kit called me on my cell. She had been out but had gotten the message that Miss Pritchard had left on her answering machine. She was on her way. Honey and I left the hospital and headed for her place.

Peter Pan greeted us at the door like she was glad to see us. I told her about the attack on Mack and she shuddered.

"You sure I'm safe here?" she wanted to know.

"Yes, only three people know you're here. Honey, myself, and Al Mack."

"Okay, don't play me now, 'cause I don't like that shit," Peter Pan said and left the room.

"We wouldn't lie to you," Honey called after her.

Honey checked the answering machine. There were four calls, one from her son Harold, one from a man who wanted to know when they were going to meet again, one from Barbara looking for Uncle Beans, and one from Melvin telling Honey that my uncle had been rushed to the hospital.

Suddenly Peter Pan appeared back in the room. Her face was puzzled and pale. "Who was that?" she asked Honey.

"Who?"

"On that answering machine that I just heard?"

Honey played the messages back.

"That's it, that's him. That's the voice of the man China Blue was speaking with," Peter Pan blurted. Her eyes were wide with surprise. "That's him, I know that voice . . . "

Honey and I looked at each other.

"You absolutely sure," Honey said.

"I swear before God," Peter Pan said crossing her finger over her heart.

I asked Honey to go to the hospital and wait for me. She agreed.

"I got work to do," I said and left.

A message on an answering machine had caused all the pieces to come falling into place. I reached my car, and checked the time. It was 11:15 P.M. I made two phone calls, one to Onion, and one to Jim Frazier in Arlington, Virginia. I hung up and thought about a big pot of good strong coffee. 'Cause the way I figured things, there was no escaping from the fact that it was going to be another long night.

*T*he man with the dead eyes lay motionless waiting. As he waited his mind drifted back to some twelve nights ago at the Tease Me Club when it all began. When two Asians broke down the door and interrupted the orgy. When the big one flung him hard into the wall. The events of that night played back in his mind like a movie.

After the two men broke into the room China Blue jumped up and started screaming at the intruders. She grabbed at a sheet on the back of the couch to cover herself. Before she could reach it, the big Asian stepped over and slapped her hard in the mouth. She fell to the floor.

"You are a traitor, you have betrayed us," he raged at China Blue with eyes bulging and the spittle of anger flying from his mouth.

China Blue looked up at him with the fury of a dragon. Her eyes had lost all their beautiful softness.

"You crazy bastard, I do what I want. You don't own me. I don't work for them no more, fuck you," China Blue screamed. "This is my party. You get out, get out." The slap of her hand against his fleshy red face sounded like a kid's cap pistol.

Like a striking cobra, the big Asian pulled a dagger from the band of his trousers and stabbed it into China's beautiful body four times, then spat full into her face. Esther screamed like a banshee, while Peter Pan scrambled to a nearby closet for safety.

The Colombian, Jesus, threw a nearby lamp at the smaller man with the gun. The lamp hit the man's hand knocking the gun to the floor. Jesus jumped onto the big Asian's back and held him tightly around the neck, cutting off his air. The smaller Asian recovered his gun and fired. The bullet hit Jesus in the arm and he let out a moan. The big Asian man was panting for air and scrambling when a hunting knife tore through his rib cage pit and punctured his lung. He turned his head and looked into the face of the man with the dead eyes. The smaller Asian positioned himself to shoot the man who had just stabbed his companion. But when he moved, Jesus dove forward and grabbed his leg, throwing him off balance. The smaller Asian fired again. This time a hole appeared in Jesus' forehead. The man with the gun looked around for the man with the hunting knife, but was too late.

The last thing the small Asian man recorded in his consciousness was the feeling of cold, hard steel slashing fire against his neck and the taste of blood filling his throat.

The man with the dead eyes smiled as he felt the familiar rush of intense pleasure that killing had always given him. Then he began to laugh uncontrollably as he grabbed Esther by the neck. In one swift movement of his powerful hands he snapped the life from her.

When the first shot was fired, Mr. Yamaguchi ran into the bathroom and locked the door. He went to the window and thought of trying to escape, but then realized he was three stories up. Instead, he just stood motionless holding his breath and listening to the sounds of uncontrollable laughter coming from the other room.

When the sounds of laughter stopped, Mr. Yamaguchi placed his ear to the door and waited ten minutes. Nothing moved. Slowly Mr. Yamaguchi unlocked the bathroom door. Cautiously, he stepped out into the living room. In his terror, he had completely forgotten that he was still naked.

Bodies. He counted five. The gruesome sight of the carnage made him vomit. Still sweating and weak, he hurriedly managed to dress himself. Just as he reached the door to leave, something moved. A sinister laugh from behind made his blood run cold. He spun around quickly. Beads of perspiration danced on his forehead then stood like raindrops on the hood of a waxed car. Mr. Yamaguchi squinted from behind his spectacles as the man with the dead eyes raised the knife and with a smile on his face, plunged it into his chest. The man with the dead eyes recalled the look on Yamaguchi's face as he awaited his angel.

The night was dull and ugly. Almost moonless. The angel pulled on her coat. She had been thinking for many hours. Now it was time to *act.* She drove to a rundown apartment building on 118th Street. She stepped out of her car, then checked behind her to make sure that she had not been followed. She entered the building and took the elevator to the ninth floor.

The man with the dead eyes answered.

He was more anxious than usual. She was more anxious to scold him.

"You didn't do it, why not?" she snapped. The angel was angry.

The man with the dead eyes didn't have the answer she wanted. He had tried and had succeeded in stabbing one man but not the other. Besides the angel never told him that the man he was sent to kill was a trained fighter. The screaming in his head had started again.

"You must kill Devil Barnett," the angel told the man with the dead eyes. "You must, otherwise, we won't be able to be together."

The man with the dead eyes wanted to be with his angel, more than he had ever wanted anything, so he agreed that he would try again.

Suddenly, the sound of a radio being turned up to nearly full blast drifted in from Mr. Willie's apartment next door. The loud radio annoyed the angel, but didn't distract her from her mission. The angel gave the man a shot of morphine and made love to him the way she always did.

"You won't ever break my heart, will you?" the angel asked the man with the dead eyes.

"Never," he answered and they continued to make love.

"When are you going to do it?" she asked.

"When do you want me to?"

"Tomorrow," she said.

I had been listening with my ear to the door and heard my own assassination being ordered. From the inside I could hear sounds of heavy breathing like two people making love. So I figured now was as good a time as any. Between the sounds of the lovemaking, I slipped the key that I had gotten from the super next door into the lock. All in one motion, I turned the doorknob, opened the door, and stepped into the room.

The couple looked up. I had counted on the sounds of the loud radio and their lovemaking to cover me. I'd been right. It was dark inside, but from a street lamp that shone through the window I could plainly see the naked woman's face. The face belonged to Barbara Simmons, my uncle's fiancée.

Barbara Simmons, the woman with the deep syrupy contralto voice of an angel. Barbara Simmons with a voice so deep, Peter Pan mistook it to be a man's voice.

Instincts took over quickly as the man threw Barbara to the floor and grabbed a hunting knife.

I clicked on the light switch and Barbara glared at me from the floor like an angry lioness. She was naked, beautiful, and had been caught totally off-guard. Exposed.

I moved deeper into the room towards her. The man with the dead eyes wielded the knife, ready to strike. Two dull thuds. The first bullet entered the man's forehead and blew out a major part of his brain, the second bullet landed in the left ventricle of his heart. The man with the dead eyes fell to the floor.

For the first time Barbara realized there was someone else in the room. She looked up and saw a white man dressed in black holding a gun in his hand. Jim Frazier lowered the weapon affixed with the silencer to his side, and the man with the dead eyes stopped breathing.

Barbara raced to the window, threw it wide open, and stepped up and out onto the windowsill.

"Don't come closer, I'll jump" she said.

I stopped dead in my tracks. "Why did you do it?" I wanted to know.

"So I could be my own woman, so that I could own something. I own a piece of that fucking building and they were trying to take it away from me. It belonged to me," she screeched from her perch. Her eyes were two fiery embers of mad malice. "My inheritance. I didn't need no landmark for no fucking tax break, I needed the money so I could be my own woman."

I guess I knew what she meant. In Onion's report to me, he had made it plain. I just wanted to hear it from the horse's mouth. I moved closer.

"I'll jump, I swear, stay back or I'll do it," she screamed.

I looked at Jim, shrugged my shoulders, then took another step forward.

And Barbara kept her promise. Her beautiful naked body careened off the building and fell nine floors to the cement below. The coroner said later that she had broken her neck on impact.

My cell phone went off. It was Honey at the hospital. She told me that the doctors had found the reason for Uncle Beans' stomach disorders. Poisoning. I explained about Barbara's swan dive and told her I had better break the news to Uncle Beans.

By 7:00 A.M. most of the people connected with the case knew what had happened. Everybody except Al Mack who was still unconscious and on the life support machine. Honey and I had breakfast with Kit, Miss Pritchard, and Uncle Beans at the hospital cafeteria.

Uncle Beans had been checked into the hospital overnight and had gotten his stomach pumped. He looked weak but was wearing his own pajamas — which he demanded, otherwise he said he would refuse to be admitted. Kit had had to go back to his house and bring them.

"There was always something I distrusted about that woman," said Miss Pritchard sternly. "People are so evil nowadays."

Kit looked over at me and smiled. Uncle Beans sat drinking tea, expressionless.

"Now what was the connection to the man doing all the killing?" Miss Pritchard wanted to know.

"Well, let me start form the beginning. Barbara Simmons was married twice before."

"She only told Daddy once before," Kit said. "Right?" she said turning to her father.

Uncle Beans didn't respond he just sipped his tea and stared out into space as we talked.

"And for good reason," I continued. "The first time she was married to a professional soldier named Gerald Holland. Holland was a sniper in Vietnam and when he was shipped back to the

States and enrolled in a deprogramming clinic in Virginia, he met and married the woman who was his psychiatric social worker named Barbara Maddox. At the same clinic she met Frank McGill, the killer, who was also a patient returning from the war. The unit she worked in was for soldiers who had been trained as assassins. Unfortunately, most of those soldiers were heroin and morphine junkies. Her job was to help deprogram them for their re-entry into society. Holland died of a drug overdose two years after their marriage and she collected a half million on his veteran's insurance. Then she married a dentist named John Simmons who lived right here in Harlem. Dr. Simmons died a few years ago from sudden heart failure and she collected on his will which was worth $1.5 million. However, most of Dr. Simmons' money was invested in real estate, in a site with landmark status. Dr. Simmons had bought an interest in the building through a business condo purchase situation. Barbara inherited the deeds to the condo property when he died. So when Sun Bright Realty started contacting the building owners through China Blue, China contacted Barbara and made an offer to buy her part of the building in cash. Her only problem was Uncle Beans, who was getting her inheritance made into a tax break, which meant that she could make money on paper, but there would be no money going directly into her pockets. She had met Uncle Beans by this time, and saw that on the one hand if she hid her true identity and ownership by having Attorney Philip Jackson represent her anonymously, and on the other hand if she could marry Uncle Beans then kill him off by poisoning, then not only would she wind up with control of the Landmark Committee but most likely with some of Uncle Beans' share in the building as well, since she would have been his wife. Two birds with one stone. Her plan for gaining control of the Committee votes and selling the building to the highest bidder was by killing off the competition."

"And to think, Daddy made her a member of the Landmark Committee," Kit said.

I continued. "It was easy to find a perfect killer since she had worked with so many. So she located Frank McGill who was in a mental institution in Detroit and signed him out, as his social worker. Then she re-hooked him on drugs and made him do her bidding.

"What about the Japanese diplomat?" asked Honey.

"He more or less just turned out to be a guy at the wrong place at the wrong time. China Blue had apparently met with Yamaguchi five days before the party to see if Yamaguchi would offer more for the building than the Koreans. A bigger deal with Yamaguchi would have meant a bigger commission for her. She had apparently told Barbara about Yamaguchi. The Koreans didn't trust China Blue, and she knew she was being watched, maybe even followed. That's why China Blue refused to meet Yamaguchi to bring him to the party herself. Yamaguchi had done deals in which he had bested Sun Bright Realty and there was no love lost between them. Peter Pan was just the beard for China Blue. China Blue must have planned to get Yamaguchi to the party and get him sexed up and high on drugs and then she would make her deal. The plan went wrong when someone working for the Koreans recognized Yamaguchi as one of their competitors in buying Harlem properties. So the Koreans put two and two together and China Blue was marked to be hit by the Catastrophic Kim brothers. Barbara didn't trust China either. She figured that if China Blue would sell out the Koreans, then China would sell her out too, but she needed China to bring in Yamaguchi. What went wrong was when the Koreans killed China Blue they triggered Frank McGill's dormant assassination mechanism, which Barbara had brought back to life."

I looked at Uncle Beans who had not said a word. There were tears streaming down his face. He was the lonely, tired picture of a ghost who haunted the museum of broken hearts. As Kit wiped away his tears with a napkin, a nurse walked over to our table.

"Mr. Barnett?" she said.

"Yes," I answered.

"You asked me to inform you if there was any change with Mr.

Mack, well he just regained consciousness and the doctor, says his condition has improved and he is going to recover.

"Thank the Lord, Thank the Lord in heaven," said Mrs. Pritchard.

"Can I see him now?"

"Yes I think so."

I stood up. "I'll be back."

"I'll come up in a minute," said Honey.

Uncle Beans had not changed his expression. A few more tears had dripped down onto his chin.

I followed the nurse out of the cafeteria feeling lighter in my heart that Mack was going to live. The sun had burned off the haze of the gray morning and had begun to shine through the window, warming up the room. Even the background pain that I had been feeling for two weeks had disappeared. The world seemed somehow a slightly better place than it had been for a while. I turned and looked back at Uncle Beans as I left the room. Him sitting there with a blank stare on his sad face, reflecting on how he had been a fool for a pretty woman. It brought to mind the words from an old blues song my grandmother used to sing around the house sometimes. "Mean Old Love Can Make A Grown Man Cry."

DEAD BY POPULAR DEMAND

Teddy Hayes' second Harlem *Noir* featuring Devil Barnett, will be available soon from Kate's Mystery Books.

Read on for an extract.

Cowboy stood at the end of the bar and looked out on the street. He was dressed in his usual outfit—a grease-spotted green plastic rain poncho, combat boots, battle fatigue pants, and a Stetson cowboy hat wrapped in a covering of brown plastic tape. The expression on his deeply lined face was one of permanent irritation. He clenched a thick dung-colored cigar between his uneven and broken yellow teeth, fidgeted with a black leather pouch strapped around his waist, and mumbled something unintelligible to himself. As he polished the glasses Duke Rodgers, the bartender, had his small portable TV tuned to a news story about a crooked politician who had been caught taking bribes in the form of prostitutes from organized crime figures. Cowboy glanced at the TV, frowned, then quickly downed half of his drink with the usual one gulp decorum.

"Damn shame," he said out loud.

Duke looked up and waited for the follow-up. With Cowboy one could never be sure. His normal commentary ranged somewhere between outright lunacy to highly intelligent. Depending on how the spirit hit him.

"They act like them politicians ain't got no dick. Hmph, they got dicks same as you and me, don't they? Sho do. Damn sho do," Cowboy stated unequivocally.

'Nuff said. It was hard to disagree with that one. Duke glanced in his direction and smiled but opted to say nothing.

"Ain't I right?" Cowboy asked again, this time in my direction. I was cleaning the beer taps.

"Yep," I said, looking up into his dirt-stained features.

As quickly as he had sprung to life, Cowboy receded back into the solitude of his personal hell as I served two customers who had just entered.

In most other parts of the world Cowboy most probably would have been considered a certified nutcase worthy of free room and board in a mental institution. But this was New York City where nutcases not only walked the streets freely, but were elected to high office, hosted programs on TV, and ran the biggest and best institutions. Besides, this was Harlem, where too long and too often people had been cheated and shortchanged. So to even things up, maybe somebody somewhere along the line decided to give Harlem more than its fair share of nutcases and make it a model community for nutcase equal opportunity. Cowboy was just a very small potato in a very large pot. He looked down at the baby stroller he always pushed around and smiled indulgently. Strapped into the baby seat was a dirty teddy bear with one eye missing. This was his son Gerald. If you didn't respect that, you could be sure to expect trouble from Cowboy. Gerald was his pride and joy, the heir to his personal madness. According to Cowboy, Gerald liked peanuts. So on some days Cowboy bought his kid a bag. Neither Duke, myself, nor Christine ever questioned him, we simply sold him the bag of peanuts.

For as long as I had owned the Be-Bop Tavern, Cowboy would come in twice a day like clockwork and order his usual — a double Jack Daniel's and ginger ale in a tumbler, no ice. He never ran a tab, always paid in cash, and was always accompanied by Gerald. One day some smart-ass had had a few too many and got up the nerve to ask Cowboy what he was doing about Gerald's education. Cowboy told him that he had Gerald in a special school that trained him how to cut the balls off people who fucked with his father. After that story went around the bar, nobody seemed too interested in Cowboy's relationship with Gerald. Cowboy generally minded his own business except for his occasional lunatic comment on life every now and then. Somehow, Cowboy just melted into the fabric that had become the Be-Bop Tavern. Nobody seemed to mind. Least of all me; he was a good customer.

It was mid-January and things had gotten back to normal after the Christmas holidays. Christine had become the manager of the bar and was doing a great job. Duke was holding down the daytime shift from 8:00 A.M. until 5:00 P.M., Benny Sweetmeat worked part-time making sandwiches during lunchtime, and Christine had hired two new people, Lonnie and Sarah, to work in the evening on her shift. Business was good.

Po Boy and Goose Jones, two old-timers, sat at their usual booth sipping coffee and reading the *Amsterdam News*. They were having a conversation with Benny Sweetmeat who was cutting bread behind the counter.

"Mohammed Ali in his day was a revolutionary man. He stood up to the whole doggone U.S. government and won," explained Goose pointing to a story in the *Amsterdam News* about the ex-heavyweight champ.

"Yeah, that's right. They tried to take everything he had. They even took away his title and his right to make a living, but the more they tried to take, the more the people loved him and the bigger he got," Po Boy chimed in.

"That just goes to show, ain't nothin' in this old world set in stone. Things change all the time in ways people can't never predict," Sweetmeat said.

"He was a real man. They don't come along like that no more," said Goose.

"Like my Daddy used to say," inserted Benny Sweetmeat. "if you gon be a man, be a man in full. Let your balls hang down like a Jersey bull."

"Quit tellin' the truth, brotha," said Po Boy holding up his glass and toasting Benny Sweetmeat's words of wisdom.

"Hey Devil," Goose called over to me. "I bet you don't remember the Rumble in the Jungle, do you?"

"Yeah I remember, Ali versus Foreman in Zaire. That's when he did the rope-a-dope. That was also Don King's first big international promotion."

Goose smiled. "I'm impressed, you know your stuff, huh?"

"Damn skippy," I smiled back.

Cowboy paid up, adjusted his hat, made sure Gerald was comfortable inside his baby buggy, and left.

Betty Logan, one of the regulars, made her way to the bar and stood where Cowboy had vacated.

"That man need to be in the crazy house," Betty said. "Give me another beer please."

I started filling another glass for her from the Budweiser tap.

"I'm gonna shock you Betty," Benny Sweetmeat said.

"What?"

"That man got a college degree and he used to own and manage lots of property right here in Harlem."

"What kind of college, the college for crazy folks?" Betty wanted to know.

"Nope, he's an accountant. If you don't believe me, ask Duke."

Betty glanced over at Duke and scowled at the thought that he was part of the joke obviously being played on her.

"He's telling the truth," Duke confirmed her questioning glance.

"What happened to him?" asked Betty, taking a swig from the freshly drawn glass of beer.

"Woman trouble," Po Boy said matter-of-factly.

"Woman trouble?" echoed Betty innocently as if it was the first time she had heard the phrase.

"Caught his woman cheating on him and it drove him off his nut."

"He was pretty well to do, too, from what I can understand," Benny Sweetmeat added.

"That's what happens when men start to thinking with that little head instead of that big head," Goose commented and adjusted his trademark which was an old style porkpie hat.

"Hmph, well I'll be damned," was all that Betty could seem to say at the thought of such a thing. Without further comment, she went back to her table and continued reading *Ebony* magazine while drinking her third beer of the day.

Winston, a crackhead and beggar who was selling stolen dresses, walked into the bar looking around. Duke spotted him before he had gotten halfway into the room.

"Not in here, you know better," was all the Duke said.

The crackhead saw Duke meant business and turned around.

Just then Shelby Green walked in. Winston stopped Shelby.

"A little something for a brotha," the crackhead said, holding out a dirty palm in Shelby's direction.

Shelby shook his head. "Fight poverty, get a fucking job."

The crackhead left and Shelby came over to where I was wiping down the bar.

"Hey Tuffy, what's up?" he greeted.

I had known Shelby Green all my life, and all my life he had called me Tuffy. Shelby Green had been a long-time friend of my family's since before I was born. He and my father had been the best of friends for over forty years. Shelby was in his sixties but appeared younger because of his high energy level and youngish features under a close-cropped bush of salt and pepper hair.

"Can we talk?" he asked me.

"Want to go into the back or sit at one of the booths?" I asked.

"Let's go in the back."

I took two coffees and we went into the back room that I had made into my office, complete with computer, filing cabinets, desk, telephone, my coveted CD jazz collection, CD player system, and a sofa.

Shelby sat on the sofa while I took a seat behind my desk. He unfolded the morning paper.

TWO DANCEHALL DOGZ FOUND DEAD IN HARLEM.

The newspaper article told of the decapitation of one rapper named SHOGUN, a.k.a Alan Leeds, and the drug overdose of another, one MAN O WAR, a.k.a Lee Mainwaring.

"One of those boys is nephew to a friend of mine."

"Sorry to hear it," I said.

"The cops notified him of the death, but when he started asking specific questions, they just turned off. You know, just another couple niggers dead in Harlem," Shelby said. "I don't know if you can do any fucking thing but, if you don't mind, as a favor to me I'd like for you to meet with him. You're smart, so I figured you might be able to give him your professional take on the thing," Shelby stated. "You know yourself, it's a bad thing to be bullshitted when your people get killed."

How well I knew.

"I ain't trying to pin no fucking roses on you, Tuffy, but you're better than any of these cocksucking Harlem detectives, hands down," Shelby said.

"These rappers must have been pretty big to make the front page," I said showing my ignorance.

"Big! Big ain't the word. The biggest on the scene right now, and making more money than God. Put it like this, these boys make more fucking money in one weekend than the average person makes all year long. All they got is one album out, but that one album has been selling like muthafucking hot cakes," Shelby explained.

We finished our coffee, and set a time to meet up with his friend later in the day. Then Shelby left.

I felt chilly. For the past few days it seemed that I had had to wear an extra layer of clothes just to stay warm. I didn't like to think about it, but I knew that the unpredictable weather could affect my sickle-cell anemia. Could send me into a crisis, too, if I'm not careful. But what could I do? Sickle-cell isn't the kind of disease you can do much about. My fate was in the hands of the gods.

I wasn't as yet experiencing any of the signs usually associated with an attack. None of the normal background pain and no fatigue. I figured that maybe what I needed was some TLC. I smiled to myself as I thought about a place where I knew I could arrange some, no problem.